MAN IN SPACE

A Short Account of War,

Space Travel,

and the Future of Us All

JOHN LINNELL

MAN IN SPACE: A Story of War, Space Travel and the Future of Us All
© John Linnell 2013, 2017

ISBN: 978-0-9949599-2-8

Published by John Linnell
16-3375 Oak St., Vancouver, BC, V6H 2L7, Canada
Tel: 604-734-0016

CONTENTS

PROLOGUE

Your journey begins with the returning to earth of the spaceship know as Mars Explorer 2 (ME-2), following the first successful manned expedition to Mars. You will meet Captain Rockheart and his crew and learn how they adapted to a 180-degree change affecting Man's total earthly existence, pursuant to the Last Great War of 2054. There was not a soul on Earth left untouched by this mega disaster. The Rockheart Chronicles takes up the first six chapters of the book, demonstrating how Man doesn't change much in attitude, in spite of wars, poverty, disease, and many other catastrophes (unexpected and unpredictable). I make no apology for highlighting and stressing the pointlessness of war and abuse of power - is there a lesson somewhere? There is another short story near the end describing a situation 10,000 years hence, mixing fact and fantasy. The rest of this literary collection is filled with poems, articles of prose and free verse, taking you down a spacey pathway, up a twisted lane - a selection of vignettes illustrating many sides of your futuristic journey - surprisingly starting and finishing with the Last Great War of 2054. Will the circle be broken?

Now read on, with hope and a prayer.

Chapter One

THE ULTIMATE FRONTIER

'SO IRONIC.'

His jaw clenched and his lips tightened as thoughts of his future ran around his head, as he further sank into his Captain's chair.

'So freakin' ironic – missed the party and lost the invitation. Stay circular, it's the best way around, they say.'

He seemed to concentrate more on the main screen in front of him. There were five screens, one on each of the corners of a square. The main one is in the middle, considerably bigger and functionally more versatile than the others.

Using the main forward camera, he had been watching an ever-increasing sized Earth - a troubling image. The top left screen told him that the Earth was 512,209 miles away. This screen was home to a library of dials, meters and charts of various shapes and sizes at the touch of a button. It was able to tell the time or distance of any and every part of the galaxy in relation to any other part. It was also home to the spaceship's interstellar positioning system (I.P.S), which would show how far the craft was from any interstellar or planetary object.

The bottom left screen could be reflective of conditions inside and immediately outside the spaceship's air quality, heat, pressure readings and all her vital signs. The two screens on the right were to do with fuel and oxygen production rates of conversion and the like. The bottom right hand screen had information regarding food, water, and all other supplies. The right hand screens were the responsibility of the other two guys in the back part of the main cabin. Each of the three crewmembers had access to a personal screen. That's Ron sleeping and Tom playing chess with himself, and in charge is Captain Charles Rockheart - all three being honours graduates from the Akademie of Astronautical Sciences in Hamburg, Germany.

The date has just changed on the top left hand screen. On Earth, it was now January 20, 2056 – 'Happy birthday Chuck!' No one was aware of Chuck's silent birthday wish to himself. After almost two years of close confinement only essential conversation was tolerated. Two spaceships known as MSE-1 and MSE-2 had taken off from the lunar space station (LSS) on January 1st, 2054 to embark on the first manned Martian Space Expedition. It was twenty days later on Chuck's thirty-fourth birthday when the last Great War started. They were successfully well on their way to the red planet - almost half a million miles from Earth and, thankfully, on automatic pilot, when an unexpected and historic chain of events took place back on Earth; adversely affecting some of the functions of both spaceships.

Both spaceships were left with no video contact with LSS or Houston Controls; only some fairly useless intermittent radio contact. They could receive radio signals but were unable to transmit. Then there were brilliant surging flashes on all screens, and minor - but intermittent computer malfunctions. This situation lasted for a few days and did not seem to affect the overall performance of the spacecraft. But nothing really worked like it did before. The bottom left screen was flashing 'PENDING E, PENDING E' continually emitting startling red letters. This automatically meant that everything was working on a sixty-five per cent energy efficiency. There should be no major problem. The ships were designed to survive long periods of time on this level of output.

So, with less than six days to go before final touchdown, Chuck flicked the remote from the hypnotic Earth picture to what they could pick up from TV satellite transmissions. Reception should be improving from now on and he sure liked those retro TV stations! There used to be hundreds, now there are only four or five - direct replays of programming fifty or sixty years old, sometimes up to a hundred years old. They were weird even back then. Present-day international news networks were few and far between - both infrequent and limited in content. It was hard to get a handle on what was happening or, indeed, on what exactly did happen. It seemed that, without warning, the Chinese People's Republic sent 200,000 highly armed troops to Taiwan and simply took over the highly populated western corridor and thus the whole island. They secured the main government buildings, the communication centers and the highly revered National Art Museum with an unabashed show of brute force. Taipei was now answerable to Beijing.

A couple of American aircraft carriers based in Okinawa and Kobe started sailing for Taiwan, but were instantly repelled by squads of Chinese fighter planes spraying deadly Stinger missiles. The U.S. lost one ship and turned the anger of the remaining carrier towards Beijing, causing a horrific fire, which completely enveloped that city. The downtown core, including Tiananmen Square, and huge stylish complexes built for long gone Olympic games were completely destroyed by a storm of missile attacks, rendering an estimated twelve million instantly dead.

Within twelve hours, two unmarked Taiwanese jet airliners took off from Mainland China, kept in regular contact with air traffic control at Vancouver International and SeaTac International Airports. Again, with no warnings, two airliners slammed into the Northwest American coast a hundred miles north and south of Anacortes Island, thus wiping out the Trident nuclear submarine base as well as all the coastal settlements for a couple of hundred miles north and south of Seattle. The lowest Canadian plate shifted and the San Andreas Fault opened up; and the ensuing tsunami took less than three hours to reach the southern Asian coast with the velocity of a jet.

Long before this would happen, a second tsunami would be sucked out and travel again at high speed the fifteen or so miles to the recently scorched Northwest coast. It was estimated that there were at least five - and maybe ten - megaton bombs on each plane - one-megaton bomb being one million times as powerful as the toys they played with a hundred years ago in Japan.

Many fires spread inland from the coastal blazes to what was left of the tinder-dry forests - the once majestic boreal forests of the north. For many years, there had been no pine, no fir, and no spruce - just dry skeletal red shafts left by merciless insects. When the first tsunami reached the central and southern Chinese coasts, there was untold death and destruction from south of Hong Kong to the north of Shanghai. Someone had taken a huge bite out of the Chinese coastline around the mouth of the Yangtze. A huge finger lake, a liquid dagger six hundred miles long, poked into the Chinese belly from the Pacific Ocean at Shanghai, whose silver skyline with giant pagodas and burly mega towers lay in ruins.

There were virtually no islands left in the North and Central Pacific, just those with substantial mountain areas - which were the only parts to survive. All coastal civilization was swept away. Some say the first tsunami was a hundred feet high. Needless to say, there were no more man-made explosions in that first week when there was nature's uncontrollable wrath to deal with.

Electricity grids collapsed in North America as well as in most of Eastern Asia if they still existed. After a week, there was a series of unexplained skirmishes in the always-fiery Middle East - the new Stinger and SKUD missiles causing havoc from Tel Aviv to Tehran continuing an increasing confrontation - Revelations indeed!! By the end of the first week, the only aircraft flying were government authorized and usually only fighter planes - air force controlled - all commercial flights having been grounded for weeks. In every country, the army and the civil guard were obvious and present, guarding government buildings and communication centres. These were the facts as Chuck understood them, though, facing the reality of up to half a billion dead was beyond his imagination at this point.

He extended his knees and pushed his shins up against the anti-weightless straps, which prevented the occupant from floating off. They were always in position unless a specific task was being performed. There were also shoulder straps restraining his body - maintaining stability. All this while he reclined in a huge dentist's chair type structure - there were three per vessel. It was where each crewmember slept, ate, read, worked, and worked-out with a specially designed system of springs.

Two vessels left LSS - only one is returning: MSE 2 was totalled in a dusty rocky Martian crash landing. We were able to position it with our IPS as we came in for our landing. When we flew in closer, it looked like a twisted metallic mess - no life left there - God knows what happened to that landing attempt. Not sure of the terrain, we didn't land there, but chose our secondary landing area - the Opportunity crater.

We had a successful eight day stay on Mars, assembling half a dozen robots, bouncing around for exercise, similar to moon walking. Mars is only slightly bigger than our moon, therefore has a similar gravitational pull. We duly and diligently collected our specimens, reenergized our fuel cells and took off. Homeward bound on automatic pilot - soon to be manually checking the top left-hand screen — soon to be reaching apogee in about three days. Then there will be two or three stabilizing orbits at about a thousand miles above the surface, and then we'll pick a spot to land. There's no more Houston, so we'll have to glide in with retro rockets firing and with whatever skills we can remember as airline pilots. There should be no problem. They designed this ship as a five star project: it maneuvers like a plane; in atmosphere it can float; it can almost find it's way home but it's lousy at making coffee…

The Earth is now looking huge and only a portion can be covered with our forward camera. But that bright, blue planet that we knew is not so bright anymore. Gigantic bands of hazy clouds crisscross Eurasia and North America at differing altitudes. There were vast stretches of desert in Central Asia, North and Central Africa, Central America, and the Middle East through northern India. We could land in the Indian Ocean, but couldn't be sure of any recovery operation sent to welcome us. So, we decided to aim for the Nullarbor Plain in Western and South Australia.

It's a convenient flight path, and with a little bit of luck - and with IPS - we might end up at Woomera; which used to be an active astronautic centre some time ago. Okay - back to work - some re-entry programming to do. His jaw further tightened as he flicked off the TV channel (presently showing an I Love Lucy rerun). Now turning to Flight Program Three reentry and landings. Ah, but don't you love the way that guy says – 'Aiyayaiyaiyaiyaiyai.'

And Chuck soon fell into a half-awake nap.

Chapter Two

HOMECOMING

"PARTY? WHAT PARTY?"

HI, THIS IS CHUCK and the way I saw it. They call me Astronauticus Meritus or even Space Pilot Supreme, travelling further than any man has gone. Now, it's just Chuck, Ron, and Tom, returning to a new world; a world looking for a lifeline - running from a deadline.

My grandfather contracted Huntingdon's Corea in his mid fifties, prompting his son - my father - to investigate a genetic enhancement program for me - vowing never to allow any of his offspring to suffer such long term debilitating symptoms. I never met him but my father would describe uncontrollable athetoid movements, which progressively plagued the old guy day and night till he died at almost eighty.

After years of research into the use of aplastic stem cells, this and many other genetic disorders have been virtually eliminated from the human genome. There are however some unpredictable side effects from such genetic manipulation, but usually positive ones.

I was human born in a hospital, in Willowdale, Ontario, Canada - a typical suburban kid, yeah right. Eh! Though I spent the first few weeks of my life in a petri dish at the Genetic Enhancement Centre in Montreal and for a short time in Atlanta, Georgia, I guess for finer tuning - I don't completely understand that subject. I was then transferred to my mother's uterus for a normal gestation period - hardly a child of passion - at least conceptually. For me, school was a breeze. So much so that friends were not easily made. I was asocial - kept to myself - read a lot but always willing and able to help someone in trouble. I was soon aware that I possessed a super photographic memory - for print, for video, for music, you name it. I could reproduce it. I was reading classic English novels at four years old. At seven years old, they said I had an IQ of two hundred and twenty. I completed an honours degree in theoretical physics and astronomy at the University of Toronto when I was seventeen.

I was neither a sportsman nor a monsieur populaire though I was naturally, physically super fit and uncannily perceptive and super responsive when found in unexpected or dangerous situations. These unusual qualities - or side effects - generated lots of respect from my peers. I was both an encyclopedia and a problem-solving machine for my equals, as well as many older than me seeking knowledge or advice. I would avidly read newspapers, technical magazines, fact books, history books, learning all I could about the world around me, and how it was changing with or without human help. I'd rather contemplate the future for this troubled race than go to a baseball game.

The fourth Gulf War of 2020 precipitated gasoline rationing in the entire civilized world - an increase in government bureaucracy. The airline industry was literally decimated and any of the few flights available were astronomically expensive. This was the situation that followed the uprising of a certain Mahmoud Hussein, the grandson of a deposed twentieth century dictator, collaborating with the remnants of a primitive, barbaric group called Al Qaeda in Afghanistan and a group of militant mullahs known as Isis breathing destruction across the Middle East. With the help of a dozen planes, suicidal pilots, and a stash of high-grade firebombs, they would methodically incinerate virtually all the large oil wells in Kurdistan, Central Iraq, Saudi Arabia and Tajikistan, with a predictable instant reaction from the Western alliance. There wasn't one Arab city that didn't feel the lethal might and supreme power that this Alliance spewed forth. Major Arab capitals were annihilated; collateral damage was enormous.

There was a gigantic 'correction' in global stock markets following the five-day holocaust of 2020. Then the corporate energy wars raged for the next ten years - fighting and bickering over control of the world's energy reserves, the use of which was becoming more and more expensive. Somehow, the fewer rich were getting richer and the many poor were getting much poorer (same old, same old). It was a bleak picture indeed, until the invention of a successful hydrogen helium fusion cell (HFC), which could be adapted for a terrestrial personal automobile-type user for powering rockets or for short or even longer space missions. The latter was my main interest. These cells could be recharged by harnessing natural sunlight into a fibrotic laser system. Oh boy, almost endless power!

I was fortunate enough to receive an honours doctorate in space medicine and engineering from the Engineering School at Princeton University. After completing this, and almost a year of training for Uncle Sam in the (USAF), I was accepted for the four year advanced course at the Akademie of Astronautic Sciences in Hamburg, Germany. This was an expanded preparation course for potential space expeditions, a practical and theoretical course. They even made use of the historic rocket site at Peenemunde, on the Baltic coast.

They practiced elementary rocket techniques, although a little different to the war games of a hundred years ago when the V2 was the fastest thing in the air. It was at this Akademie that I met Ronald O'Reilly, and Tomasso Sarkissien, both with the rank of Captain.

Ron was a soft-spoken Irishman, sandy-coloured hair and relatively small in stature. His five foot eight was not even a hundred and eighty pounds - but tough and strong as an ox, though you'd never know it by his velvet voice and comfortable countenance. You'd never miss his dry, gut busting sense of humour with lightening quick answers, often having a sting at the end, but then he is a Scorpio (I knew it!). Tom had an Armenian dad and an Iranian mom and was born in Manchester, England. Hyperkinetic, he was always smiling, always moving, always doing something good in any situation at hand. A brilliant mind, he could do integral calculus in his head in seconds - blow you away - but never exuding anything but calmness and confidence - two capable guys, reliable and sensitive. After finishing at the Akademie, the three of us were accepted for training at the Busch Space Centre in Northern Florida - about halfway between Cape Kennedy and Tallahassee, still on the coast.

This space centre was built about twenty years ago primarily for the Lunar Settlement Program. With recent advances in space technology and rocket propulsion, a massive expedition was begun in 2035 in order to start a permanent settlement on the inhospitable lunar surface. Thankfully, the richer nations of the world have been placing more money in this dream - and also in successful geothermal production - rather than funding pointless wars for questionable motives; these being either territorial or monetary in nature.

We three took our first lunar trip in 2050, staying at the lunar colony - now well established - for six months. At that time there must have been almost 200 people living there - including a dozen or so couples with a dozen or so growing kids - growing active, happy and healthy. I couldn't help thinking how those kids seemed to be living in a mix of Disneyland and Club Med - except there was no going home. While on this trip we met three others - a Russian, a German and an American who with Tom, Ron and myself had also been selected for a future Martian expedition.
There was minimal social contact or meaningful exchange. We were there for a reason, for a job, and not to enjoy the continually expanding facilities at the Lunar Space Station. These included a half-Olympic-size swimming pool, surrounded by exotic tropical plant life and even some small birds, irrigation streams and waterfalls, amusement and games rooms, and workout areas and were covered by a mammoth, energy-saving geodesic dome. Surrounding and attaching to the main dome were dozens of Quonset type huts - for supplies, development, living quarters and other services necessary for the running of an average lunar suburb.

The whole complex was built on the edge of the Sea of Tranquility, using minicrater formation for protection against frequent meteor storms and solar flares. About five kilometers away is the main take off and landing pad with labs, space control equipment, tracking tower and telescopes. There'll be a shortcut tunnel joining these two outposts - probably in a year or so.

It was from this lonely and eerie lunar landscape that we took off on January 1st, 2054 using the so called slingshot method - to throw us from Earth orbit to Mars - about forty-five million miles away. We could only take off over a forty-eight hour period per month, that is, when the moon is at apogee (the furthest point from the center of the earth). We were tossed like a rock through space heading for another lonely eerie world: the red planet. All that seems so long ago, as I relax into my semi slumber.

"Looks like we just passed perigee." Ron's dulcet tones fluttered in my headset, diplomatically interrupting my shallow sleep. Can't wait to have deep sleep-in Saturday morning style - without headphones. I glanced at the lower left screen - 0.4 degrees to 0.5 degrees. This value will gradually increase until we reach our apogee and then decrease to zero at perigee - all orbits are elliptical, and as long as we keep our speed below the velocity of just over 18,000 miles per hour or seven miles per second, we should remain in our present orbit 1075 miles above the earth, and about fifty or so miles further out when apogee is reached. The ship would circle the earth twice and then wait for further instructions.

So, I loaded the IPS coordinates of Woomera, and instructed our obedient vessel to commence descent. We should make almost two more full orbits while gradually descending giving us a real good look at Mother Earth not seen for two years by us. We instantly notice a grey haze everywhere over land and sea, with those crisscross cloud formations throughout the Northern Hemisphere. However, there were no clouds over the Arctic Ocean. In fact there was hardly any ice in the Arctic or anywhere near Northern Canada and Northern Siberia.

This once tundra and permafrost now appeared greeny-brown. The further north, the greener Central Asia and east to the Chinese coast, was. It was as if the Gobi desert had expanded in all directions - different dull shades of yellow somehow looking super dry. There were darker shades where lakes used to be. There was no Caspian Sea, just a yellow-brown shaded area, with a bright yellow strip in the middle. The Aral Sea appeared just as lifeless. There were patchy dark areas along the southern China coast into the Malayan Peninsula, but absolutely nothing from the Yangtze to the Po Rivers - just a fractured coastline and terrain that looked like a moonscape - some faint urban glows much further inland. Northern and central Africa was that same beige to khaki shade all the way to India. There was no colour variation in North and Central America, no green until the far north of Canada, where apparently they now grow peaches and pineapples. The Pacific coast west of the Rockies was unrecognizable, the landmass having that lifeless grey lunar look about it - no snow on the Western Cordillera, north or south.

Apart from the far, far north, the only green and presumably fertile areas were the southern tip of South America into Tierra del Fuego and southeastern Australia. Look at the Antarctic - no clouds - half a dozen islands of ice - is there life anywhere?

We've completed two orbits, one a nighttime sweep over North America - we could make out only dimly-lit urban centres on the eastern half of the continent, nothing like the trillion light bulb extravaganza we were used to seeing, especially illuminating the United States. Now there were simply no lights on the western half.

Guess it's time to go down, once more around the block and a gradual turn to port, just south of Madagascar... wow...now we're decelerating - 4G, 3G, 2G....straighten her up there's the Nullabor Plain...looks hotter than hell down there...Adelaide coming up.....sharp port about two hundred miles and, as if by magic, we've arrived ten thousand feet above Woomera, hovering, the automatic pilot waiting for a further command.

I checked to find the exact coordinates of where we are and where that runway is, push go, and then relax into the final approach - flick on manual - ready to stick handle my way over the last two miles of terra firma. What a feeling

- retro rockets on. What a trip. What a ship. She made it. Everything worked - even the undercarriage with species of red dust still clinging to one of the wheel axles.

....Brakes on stationary mode....We had successfully landed. About five hundred yards from what looked to be like a control tower from another age and a few huts surrounding it. We waited about fifteen minutes for pressure to stabilize. Then we dispensed with our protective pressure suits - worn for the descent, and always a major job to robe and disrobe - turn off all systems apart from those which are needed to reenergize our HFC - time to open the airlock. So we did. We hadn't been aware of any movement or sound outside, looking at each other in disbelief, after a full silent minute, we heard our first human sound.

"Good day, mate, why don't ya come down?"

Three bodies wobble unsteadily towards the exit - three animated faces appeared in the doorway.
"Good day to you", I replied - forcing as natural a smile as possible, but emitting friendliness.

"Dusty Miller at your service - Sir.", said the stranger, with a mock salute.

"You don't look like UFO types to me." His broad grin revealed a long-term lack of dental care. He wore a wide, soft brimmed cowboy hat, one side pinned up, a plaid shirt, and jeans which had never seen a washing machine, and I'm sure could stand up by themselves. He had wheeled up a rickety old staircase from somewhere and we clambered down.

"No," I said. "We just got back from Mars."

"Yeah, right." He was plainly incredulous,

"And I was skiing on the Snowy mountains this morning ain't no snow there since the war. Never mind, come on in, have a beer. What's that you got, family album?" Tom was carrying a folder full of photographs of Mars, of the moon, of the Earth from way out in space.

"No, just some holiday memories," Tom smiled. "Show you later."

We trudged to the main building, we three obviously ataxic, getting used to the heaviness of the Earth's gravitational pull - this walking business is hard work. We passed through the reception area into a large lounge containing at least six chesterfields, or sofas, very old colonial style, but I'm not sure which colony; but made for hotel use. Everything was dry and woody and dusty - very apt. The leather on the sofas was cracking and starting to split at the corners. The colours, originally pastel, were faded. Photographs covered the walls - mainly groups of people, some aircraft or rockets in the background, some with pilots in uniform - all looked like taken many years ago.

"So what happened to the rockets and stuff?" Ron enquired. "I thought this was an active centre still."

"No," says Dusty. "Not since the war, that's when I bought it cheap - now I rent it out to city slickers who want to know what the outback feels like. I was caretaker here before the war and caretaker here since the war. Not many people come by. Got two staying here right now. You'll see them in the morning."

There were a dozen or so cabin-like structures spread out around the main building interspersed with tiny sporadic groves of stunted eucalyptus trees. All the healthy ones were about two feet high, the older tall ones looked quite sick; dried out with hardly any leaves.

"How come no bugs," I noticed.

"Too hot now." Says Dusty. "We'll have a few come winter, there's been a lot less bugs."

"Since the war." Ron nodded and completed the statement with a deadpan face.

"Yeah." Dusty grinned. "Things sure have changed, so where have you been flying from - really now?"

The folder of photographs was on a long coffee table. Tom gently pushed it to Dusty.

"Check it out" said Tom. And we three as one stood up to attention, and, myself leading, recited our name, number and rank, saluted in unison, and sat down smiling.

Dusty hit the side of his head with his hand, and slugged a mouthful of beer down.

"Now I remember. They lost track of you guys. Crashed or something?" he questioned himself. "Was that before the war?"

"I think the war came after we left." Tom's voice was almost musical and I wondered if Dusty had any memory of events before the war.

"My God, you should have seen it," said Dusty. "I'm glad I weren't there, saw some TV shots at the time, just saw a little bit, just a couple." His voice trailed into memory land.

"I saw aerial photos of Northern California and Oregon - two days after." His commentary became deadly serious.

"That's more than five hundred miles from where they hit. It looked like everything was melted - and hardened - you know - which I guess it was. Miles of fried wilderness. It weren't so bad east of the Rockies - well least till the radiation started, just took days. Some survived, millions died – painfully, no escape."

He stopped with a tortured look on his face. "It must have been bloody awful. It weren't bad down here, just got hotter - specially Queensland and Darwin way - you know - with a giraffe long neck and no tail, crocs giving birth to dead crocs - cockroaches nigh a foot long."

"I seen 'em." he exploded and calmed down.

"Still not much radiation down here." His face lightened slightly. I seem to remember some obscure Bertrand Russell essay describing how atomic radiation would not cross the equator - or at least past the tropics - maybe the old guy was right after all.

Dusty continued. "We don't import food anymore from Europe or from Asia - hardly any fish, no more - contaminated anyway. All our stuff is grown in Victoria and Tasmania - you know - especially where the Murray meets the Murrumbidgee River." He gets excited.

"Beautiful down there - green - lush - subtropical - growing pineapples and mangos. Y'know what - they're growing coffee beans on top of the Snowy Mountains - huge crop, first year. Can you believe it? Makes more money than skiing. We got lots of stuff - we're okay - we don't need any immigrants. Did you guys lock up that plane of yours?"

Three heads shook in unison.

"You better do it," he warned. "There's abos around - they'll steal anything - they're not the same as us you know."

Tom started to rise. "Finish your beer first." Dusty interjected.

The old caretaker talked nonstop - I don't think he has much practice at it. He's probably in his fifties but looks twenty years older - dry wrinkled skin with eczema type lesions on his forehead, neck and forearms. The lager was cold, sparkling and refreshing, Fosters of course. Dusty takes an excursion into Adelaide every two weeks to pick up his supplies - beer and any other essentials he might need, including boxes of dehydrated food (just like home). He has access on his property to a reliable artesian well - a main reason this spot was chosen for the Woomera testing range a hundred years ago.

"Let me get you boys some tucker. It's almost sundown and - well, I guess you're staying the night, eh?"

We offered apologetic thanks, locked up the ship, found three cabins, close to the main building, put a bag of nightly essentials on the bed of each cabin and went back to the main lounge to partake of some tucker; the same dehydrated tucker we'd been eating for two years - but his water tastes better.

He shuffled over to a desk on which there was an antique looking podmaster domestic control panel (DCP), Ron smiled with affectionate recognition, remembering the original iPod and iPhone, remembering the gadgetry craze in the early part of the century when he was a kid. Dusty then proudly pushed a button and, low and behold, the lights dimmed and a set of wall curtains parted revealing a huge ancient plasma TV screen.

"We got three channels here", he stated, like the bearer of hot news.

"Retro TV, retro movies, and Aussie TV whenever they feel like it. Or whenever it's working. Let's see." He flicked the TV on and there was Rickey Ricardo, Ai aiai ai....

Tom rolled his eyes heavenwards and mimed the completion of that classic hook line after Dusty had flicked over to the movie channel explaining his actions as - "Can't stand that guy. Now, here's a good movie - you guys will like this - Space Odyssey 2001 by Arthur C. Clarke."

We three suddenly became tired and politely retired.

Chapter Three

On the Road Again
"Dry Martini to Go Please"

IT WAS UNCANNILY STILL AND QUIET when I slipped into sleep. That's because there are no crickets, no cicadas. I sleepily mused on this thought and in moments I was gone. It was just as peacefully quiet when I woke ten hours later. It was one real sleep at last. The next day, found my brain buzzing with the contemplation of our present situation and how it could unfold.

I lay there still and eyes closed for what seemed like many minutes, attempting to put the broken pieces together inside my unusually confused head. And, not for the first time in my life, wondering why I was there - here, in the middle of nowhere - from one inhospitable environment to another. I slowly opened my eyes and looked out the window at a pale blue sky covered with a thin silky blanket of grey high cloud; that haze was everywhere.

It was 7am local time - this was the readout from my personal communication device – (PCD), Local time was about the only function I could be sure of from the once multifaceted device, an instrument - about the size of a pack of cards and attached to my belt. I used to be able to send and receive anything almost anywhere there was video space net (VSN). All information was a touch screen away. VSN is the expanded version of the old Internet, but a lot more transparent and informative, and potentially more abusive, but I guess you could say that about any total system; you know how they said absolute power corrupts… absolute power corrupts absolutely.

Like the rest of the MSE-1 and its flawed communication system, we received no communication for over two years. My PCD has followed suit - nothing - zippo - nada. No contact with Edwards Air Force base or with Busch Space Centre. It was starting to sink in - the vastness of the events of two years ago and the indescribable consequences on humanity. Looking out the window towards the main building, I saw the windsock impotently flutter in the gentlest of breezes – symbolic!! I guess we were lucky to find this place - and - Dusty, the original ocker, such an incorrigible country bumpkin, though somewhat lovable.

"Good day, Chuck, cap'n, sir." Dusty's nasal tones surprised the ancient intercom speaker - as well as my still sleepy self.

"Breakfast is in half an hour and we leave for Adelaide by car in one hour."

I was amazed at the pressure of the running water in the shower cubicle - did that ever feel good, my first terrestrial shower since who knows when! I bopped around the tiny bathroom areas with my loaded toothbrush, like a little boy excited at the novelty of being in my very first hotel room - checking out tiny and empty closets, and the set of drawers, which contained a predictable unopened Gideon's bible. I met Tom and Ron outside the main building, all three considerably more awake than the previous evening. We viewed and examined photographs and other objects of interest lying around. There were few, until Tom appeared from an anteroom, holding a five-foot long tubular object.

"A didgeridoo!" I exclaimed. "Can you play it?", I gently mocked. Tom blew into it. Ron and I took turns and blew but still nothing happened. We sat around the lounge waiting for a final call to food. We'd now run out of entertaining diversions.

"Five minutes - won't be long." Then Dusty was gone, only to reappear in full kitchen uniform leading the other chef.

"I'd like you to meet Slim." Slim shuffled out of the kitchen.

His nickname, an obvious misnomer - as demonstrated by his excess avoirdupois. He was slow moving and somewhat directionless, though he did end up at the side of the room where the didgeridoo was, picked it up, and sat down in a squatting position, with the doo resting on the floor in front of him. He blew into the instrument by pumping his stomach muscles like a strong bellows. The sound produced was huge and sent shivers down my spine - something like bag pipes. He stopped blowing instantly when Dusty yelled

- "Okay" from the kitchen and appeared with a tray-full of plates: three for our table and two for another prepared table.

Slim hovered from table to table, straightening cutlery - silver, indeed - adding condiments and the like - linen napkins, to boot. The eggs were real - looked and tasted good. The bacon was grey looking and was a long time from pig but still tasted good. The bread was very white, except where toasted, and I guess the pile of mush was an attempt at old style hash browns - greasy but filling. There was a jar of orange marmalade, apparently manufactured by appointment to HM King William V. There was instant coffee, sugar and "Sorry, no milk today, but you're welcome to a beer." Such was Dusty's generous explanation. "Don't get milk very often these days - contaminated - high levels of Strontium 90".

The other table arrived hand in hand, and sat down hand in hand, with a cursory nod and "Good day" in our direction. One pair of eyes remained glued to the other; had to have been a honeymoon couple - or an elopement - about twenty-five years old, blond, pale, dry skin - kinda nervous looking. Obviously wondering about we three, and that strange looking airplane thing parked outside, looking like a zooped-up version of the old Boeing 727, but with wings a lot more swept back and much smaller tail unit. I wonder if they had any idea what MSE-1 was all about.

"We'll go in the jeep", says Dusty. The magnesium battery of his four-wheel drive vehicle was already charged. Dusty continued: "We'll stock up with some vittles, then go and visit my friend Bernard - he's a ham radio buff - knows lots about most things - you know."

All four climbed into the cab, I being the last to enter, stopped for a few seconds and listened to the silence surrounding me - deafening. I was so used to the constant hum of the spacecraft's systems. The lack of any noise was disconcerting to say the least, as if something was wrong, something was not here.

'You got that right, Chuck.' (My inner voice). I finally got into the cab and we drove off, gliding down a secondary road, as these bat mobiles seem to do very well - gliding silently.

After about twenty miles, we hit the main north-south highway at a T-junction, with a north south signpost - Alice Springs 440 miles north - Adelaide 190 miles south, so we turned right and glided for about three hours.

Dusty was constantly fiddling with the dashboard podmaster, unsuccessfully trying to get some radio signal from somewhere, but receiving nothing from anywhere, apart from various tones of static white noise. We were impressed with the never ending dried out and stunted vegetation, scantily covering hot sandy dunes. A north-south telephone line was the only other evidence of any human life… There was not one other vehicle on the road in either direction. The early morning had been a pleasantly cool fifty degrees F. By eleven o'clock and much closer to the coast, it was a humid 95 degrees Fahrenheit - should hit a hundred and ten by three o'clock.

Suburban Adelaide was not dissimilar to suburban Southern California of a hundred years ago, just as sprawling, looking like a high-end work camp with no modernizing, upgrading or even painting.

There were numerous one-story bungalows, small and large, many of which were surrounded by dilapidated white picket fences, separating one neat lot from another. Three or four-story small apartment blocks were sporadically interspersed, housing a lower stratum of workers. There grass was greener in the developed urban area - irrigation - many more flowers and butterflies - saw one with a ten inch wing span, flashing exotic tropical colours. There were few people walking around until we got to the downtown area, where people were moving about as if in a country town. There was little traffic, no holdups at traffic lights - more gliding bat mobiles than older I-C engines and, again, unexpectedly quiet. Everyone, without exception was wearing long sleeves and long pants or displaying wide-brimmed hats or holding umbrellas. Most people were sun-drenched blond, with the same pale, arid-look about their expressionless expression. Many had psoriatic lesions on the face and neck. We parked outside a nondescript building calling itself South Australia Supplies Ltd. Where Dusty would replenish his diminishing vittles.

"Bernard's house is only about four blocks away." Dusty was enthusiastic. "Let's go see who he's been talking to. He's sure to have a beer ready."

Bernard Johnson was a retired ship's radio and radar engineer, who immigrated to Australia from England over forty years ago. He was a small wizened man but rather spry for his age and certainly alive in his mind. His piercing bird-like eyes were the main feature of a face whose forehead expanded high and wide to a greying fringe of hair at the back, traveling from ear to ear. His head looked almost too heavy for his modest five foot four frame. His voice on the other hand was large, confident and knowledgeable, and indeed, the beer was soon served with welcoming alacrity. He was seriously interested in our Martian escapades, having good knowledge of the original trip.

However, it seemed that the last Great War had made a severe mess of many things, especially in the northern hemisphere. He recounted how the whole western American coastline from Vancouver Island to Southern California has shifted maybe a few feet, the resultant physical damages varying from severe in the south to catastrophic in the north. There was nothing left from San Francisco, California to Vancouver, Canada. Millions were instantly fried by the flashes, millions more swept away with the tsunamis. Those who survived in the surrounding areas like Southern California, the western States and northern Mexico would regret not having perished in the first few minutes.

Most highways and bridges were impassable. Uncontrollable fires everywhere - electrical grid gone for the western half of the continent. After a few weeks there, hordes of starving people with severely acute radiation sickness, mostly armed with handguns, were roaming the countryside. "The army's in control there now," said Bernard, "but they say radiation sickness is spreading, and spreading to Europe too - from east and west."

"Not too bad down south here. They say the safest place in the world is South Island New Zealand and Tierra del Fuego in South America. I heard they're reconstructing the space net - I think without China. There was so much destruction, especially in Asia: huge industrial parks, dams, coalmines, and energy generating stations, factories, underwater cables - all gone. Thank god for landlines. But it's still very difficult to make overseas telephone calls. Sometimes there's a three day wait and if you're not there when they call you, you don't get it - one chance only; and when you finally do make a connection, it's like talking to someone in Pitcairn Island - like they're talking from a faraway bathroom."

We three sat wide-eyed as we let Bernard ramble. He continued: "There was a sharp increase in water pollution levels after the war - on land and in the ocean. For instance, the striped jellyfish has grown as big as the box jellyfish - bigger than a fridge, with twenty to thirty foot long tentacles - lethal. These creatures are surrounding Australia and what's left of the islands up north - used to be only north east coast, now they control the ocean from Australia to Japan - feeding on human junk of all sorts and garbage that gets in their way - as well as many smaller fish. Their giant tentacles reach up to the shore in shallow waters and lagoons. There's no ocean safe for swimming - there's no fish worth eating, but I guess it's put a stop to the refugee boats coming from South Asia - no safe place to beach – over-loaded boats capsizing - everybody dies."

"Well, we don't need them Pakis here," snorted Dusty, the hairs on his red neck bristling in the afternoon heat.

"Oh, you're so pure," retorted Ron, with only a touch of gentle sarcasm flavouring his cutting remark. Tom, however didn't change his composure; his Armenian toughness and Persian aloofness putting him in a place above the conversation. I enquired of Bernard about the lunar station. As far as he could recollect, there was a flight from the moon bringing back families who chose to return, but it was the choice of a hundred or so to stay up there. They have water purification plants, oxygen production systems, and food and other supplies to last them for years. There were no more moon trips planned as far as he knew.

"Our crop production here is down about thirty percent this year over last. Cows are producing less milk and it starts to be infected. Merino sheep are not mating or reproducing - they're down fifty percent. We've lots of artesian water, clean so far, and lots of dehydrated food. That's better than most of the world. Increasing droughts in northern Africa have made one monster dust bowl there - quite uninhabitable. Melting glaciers in the Himalayas and Andes are causing flash floods and landslides. Chronic drought in northern India has destroyed the mustard crop - for the second year, no wheat in China."

"There's minimal north-south interaction - we don't want to go up there, and we don't want them coming down here. You know there are olives and citrus fruits in Northern Europe, grapes in Siberia. There's thick smog most of the year in northern urban centres and hotter than hell in summer. There's no more permafrost and the peat bogs of Siberia are oozing methane by the ton. Tropical and subtropical areas get floods and landslides regularly. New cancers getting diagnosed everyday. Africa is consumed with cholera, malaria and AIDS, as is Southeast Asia. They just don't have clean water, or sufficient food - or medicines - we're lucky, down here." He paused with a long deep sigh.

"So, what do you three intend to do?" The old man's eyes narrowed as he studied each of us slowly one by one. The other two looked at me. I said, "We should have a meeting soon."

"Well, why don't you have your meeting here and now?" piped up Dusty.

"Then I can go and load up my stuff and, when I get back here, we can have some tucker, then hit the trail home."

"Sure," said Bernard, reaching for his domestic control panel, and after some deftly administered commands: "Dinner will be in twenty five minutes," and he relaxed into his chair, not intending to move for twenty-five minutes.

"There's no point in you guys going to the communication centre, you won't get access to any relevant information or computer even if they work. You don't have a Personal Security Number (PSN) or chip - everyone's got one - you wouldn't get past the blonde behind the glass, let alone the two armed goons at the top of the steps." His thin lips almost extended to his ears in a wide grin and his beady eyes almost twinkled.

"In fact you're bloody aliens."

"I vote that we have a meeting." Tom's voice was unusually urgent.

"Right." said Tom and Ron in unison.

Bernard relaxed back in his rocking chair, clasped his hands across his modest belly and closed his eyes; now he's put the cat amongst the pigeons.

"He's right, you know." There was an element of whimsy in Ron's tone, "So, Cap'n, what do we do?" They both looked at me expectantly.

"What do we do about the specimens?", I deflected the question swiftly. There were three hermetically-sealed stainless steel cases weighing about seventy pounds each, full of carefully gathered samples of soils, rocks, and dust, Martian style, separated and categorized. I continued:

"There is a reliable university in this town, Flinders University - and they used to have an active astronautical engineering department."

"It's now only astronomy." Bernard's eyes didn't open with his comment:

"Same professors though."

"Well," I concluded. "I think we should talk to the university people and see if they will accept our samples in good faith. At least our specimens would find a secure and environmentally controlled situation - at least temporarily. I sat back in my rattan chair. It creaked as I lay back and waited for reaction. Dinner was the next comment. We could hear Dusty's boots stomping up the wooden front steps.

"Strewth, mate." He staggered in, sweating. "She's hotter than a…." He turned away from us in mock embarrassment, "Oops, sorry."

Then, to the dozing Bernard, "Got a beer, mate?"

A beer appeared, as if by magic, on the kitchen counter top, already uncapped, a victim of Bernard's touch control on his DCP.

So eat and run - we had to and we did; it would be dark by the time we arrived at the disused air base and the plan was to bring the cases to the university the following day, and then make plans to leave this place as soon as possible, to where I don't know. Anywhere in the northern hemisphere was seriously uninviting to all of us. Permanent residence in a southern hemisphere outpost was just as uninviting.

As we drove north, we had a front row view of an incredible sunset over the western desert. Sheets of pinks, mauves, purples and reds, turning to azure and deep blue tints darkening indigo to blue-black and finally black. We were latitude thirty-five degrees south, so the whole light show barely took half an hour - that brilliant ball of sun fire slowly descending behind this vividly colorful silk curtain, changing shades and folds every few seconds until there was no colour left. It was definitely night when we arrived back at the base. The few lights illuminating the out buildings did not distract from the blackness of the sky, and, although it was still almost thirty degrees Fahrenheit temperature, there was a surreal chill to that dense blackness, to that moonless night, strangely devoid of stars. The ramshackle buildings looked cold and stark. Somehow a night on Deimos seemed more attractive.

Chapter Four

PERSONA NON GRATA
"TIME TO GET OUT OF HERE"

DIDN'T SLEEP MUCH THAT NIGHT, had the buzzing brain syndrome again - why, why, why. Why didn't those idiot politicians of half a century ago foresee the potential dire consequences that would arise from continued trade conflict and competition for market share and it's ramifications, between a Euro American group on one side and a Chinese-South Asian group on the other. Somewhere in the middle of this, Muslims still hated Jews, and the Judo-Christian block still insisted their God was the right God and the Pope was still laying claim to infallibility on matters of the spirit, irrespective of the socioeconomic effects of his edicts. I guess there was a long fuse on that keg of dynamite.

However, I digress - back to me, and now.

The following day we arrived at Adelaide about three hours before our appointment at the University. We started to feel familiar with that deserted strip of boring blacktop. We were using a larger biodiesel type of truck with which to transport our specimen cases to a better home. Tom and Ron had noticed that when transferring the cases from MSE-1 to the truck, someone had moved the old rickety stairway we had used for descending and ascending to the main door. This was about four meters above the ground, even when the craft was in the horizontal position. There were no other signs of interference but someone had been investigating. Indeed it was curious how the pale blonde couple had given us the real cold shoulder at breakfast. Dusty was unusually quiet on the highway trip.

Slow and deliberate, I ventured:

"We need to get some supplies," hesitantly, "before we leave."

"She'll be 'right." Dusty sounded resigned, knowing we had no money, or any identification worth showing, but it was no problem. We procured some essentials enough to last we three a few days. Our water purification plant had lots in reserve and the oxygen regeneration system was working just fine.

The essentials we chose were such gourmet delights as dehydrated vegetable soup, dehydrated beef or chicken stew, dried eggs, dried fruit juice concentrates and the like. We allowed ourselves a bag of candies each for an overdue treat. I chose liquorice Allsorts - Bassett's of course - Tom and Ron each chose Mentos. We were fresh out of frozen bread mix - an excellent bread - whole-wheat - cereal substitute - they'd never heard of it at this store. Dusty had no qualms about using a plastic card and identification chip at the checkout, but then he fitted in, whereas we were getting quizzical looks from the general populous in the store and on the street. We received sidelong glances from bland expressionless faces wandering aimlessly about, with no apparent or at least urgent purpose to attend.

We walked on to Bernard's house for a visit, relieved to reach there, after four or five blocks of being stared at.

After knocking. "Come on in." was the answer from deep within his house. We entered the closed but unlocked front door and followed the voice to what appeared to be an office or study-type room. One and a half walls were shelves of books, mainly technical, books on radio and radar engineering, ham radio technology, geology, astronomy, a whole shelf of historical books from Shakespeare to Churchill to Plato, stacks of technical magazines.

And the wall was full of small containers holding screws, nails, multi-shaped brackets, electrical plugs and adaptors, lengths of electrical cables hanging on hooks, everything neat and tidy. Seated at a large desk in front of a complicated looking consul sporting earphones, a mouse in one hand and a remote in the other, was Bernard.

"Come in, come in" with urgency, and he beckoned to a few chairs around.

"I just got through to London. Expecting a reply any minute." He then removed his headphones, directing the sound to a small wall speaker.
"Come in 2LO Cock, over. Come in 2LO Cock, over."

Silence - waiting - watching and immediately after a third

similar signal was transmitted, two green lights began flashing and an unusual crackling buzz came forth from the wall speaker. Bernard quickly moved a potential meter slider, down to zero and pushed a couple of buttons; the buzzing stopped and

"2LO Cock calling WOGGAWOGGAROO over, 2LO Cock calling WOGGA WOGGAROO, over."

Bernard held a lever down and,

"WOGGAWOGGAROO calling 2LO Cock, over."

"How is your winter's day, any snow down there yet? Over."

"It's mid summer here, 110 degrees, over."

"I figured that," came the distant voice. "Just a little envious. We're just recovering from our third freezing windstorm of the season up here, 200 miles an hour winds blowing across Russia and Scandinavia, causing havoc with our East coast flatlands. We just caught the tail end of it, over."

"It's very, very hot down here but still quite free of radiation sickness." Bernard continued. "I have the three Martian astronauts with me. Don't ask me to explain that; they want to know what life is like in England now, over."

Crackle, crackle, buzz, buzz followed by some frantic button pushing, then - "It's hell here; all hospitals are full to overflowing, now doctors are dying. The Thames River is a huge lake west of Windsor and very polluted. The North Sea has eaten up most of northern East Anglia - there are no fens left - what was marsh is now tidal water. Norwich, Colchester, Ipswich are connected by elevated highways, twenty feet high, and hopefully protected from the elements by huge concrete levies. All they do in the long run is push the water somewhere else. Storm surges are spreading far inland, causing chaos in lower coastal area seven up to Scotland. They say the White Cliffs of Dover are wearing away - victims of chronic erosion."

The dispassionate voice continued.

"At least the windstorms blow away the freezing fog. Apart from these winter windstorms, everything is hot or superhot - the olive crop in Yorkshire was good this year - Kiwi fruit yield improving - huge banana trees in the South of France. All foods, petrol, biodiesel products, are rationed. Nothing may be purchased without the appropriate voucher - complete government control. Police and Home Guard are armed with nerve guns and use them. Sporadic spontaneous food riots, especially in the large cities up North. The lights of Blackpool have been out for two years. Don't' come for a holiday, over."

His words started to fade into the crackle; Bernard jiggled some knobs and inquired.

"How is your health? Over."

The reply sounded both strained and pained.

"A little worse, losing more weight, follow the ration books, keep to yourself, avoid the security police, that's the best anyone can do, over and out."

"WOGGAWOGGAROO to 2LO Cock, reception poor, try same time tomorrow, over and out."

The intense crackling muffled the reply, drowning the fading call signal. Bernard switched the consul off, and swung his chair around, so to be facing us.

"So you want to go to England?" he playfully mocked.

"I don't think so," said Ron, "Sounds much worse than here - I mean, not that here is..." His voice trailed into nothing and he looked at the floor; every hour the realization of our predicament became glaringly obvious.

"You know what I mean," Tom concluded. Bernard lowered his voice, and with deliberate meter, he played at lecturing us.

"I think you three should avoid any encounter with the security people. You're from the North, You're in Australia illegally, you've got no PSN, no passport or identity chip - or anything you might need these days. Look at you, you fit in like a square cork in a round hole. We looked at each other, identical long sleeved T-shirts, off white, regular issue, old NASA stock, identical dark blue sweat pants, regular issue, as above. Ron and I had grown quite unkempt longish hair, though Ron's forehead was much higher than mine; Tom's hair was cut a little close, but was still unruly - none of us were trained as hairdressers. We looked like a retro-rock music group on vacation.

"We gotta get outta here, let's go to the university," I said rising, acknowledging Bernard's hospitality and advice with a respectful bow and off we drove, easily finding the university downtown - kinda thought it might be somewhere near a generously treed boulevard called University Drive. It also wasn't difficult to figure out the astronomy building either - must be that three story building with the satellite dishes and radio telescopes on top. We slowly chugged around to the back of the building, whereupon two big garage doors swung open, allowing us to drive into an enormous storage area. For the entire world, we could have been in a scene in a very early James Bond movie. However, back to reality. There were three important looking academic types waiting for us. We introduced ourselves by rank and number, the middle taller man with the Einstein-like haircut and glasses, held his hand out for the triple shake.

"Pleased to meet you. Dr. Edward M. Carlsberg. Edward equals M. Carlsberg squared, ha, ha, ha."

He must have quipped this corny line a thousand times in his academic career. We three smiled diplomatically, the other two remained expressionless, rolling eyes heavenwards. One of Dr. Carlsberg's assistants had a shifty mistrusting look about him, like he never looked anyone in the eye, and his conversation was limited to -

"Mmm, mm, ah, yes uhu." Or some other ineffectual response to someone else's remark - certainly didn't make one feel comfortable.

We then discussed under what environmental conditions our specimen cases should be kept - and for how long etcetera - they had just the space. Carlsberg pushed a buzzer on the wall and three identical store clerks arrived, dressed in brown overalls, and each driving a mini batmobile, or motorized trolley, maximum speed ten miles an hour, but can turn on a dime and could carry up to five hundred pounds of cargo behind the driver's seat. I guess they must be union employees for they each loaded up one case and disappeared down a corridor, deeper into the building.

We started to follow and then, a couple of meters down the corridor, turned into Carlsberg's office, whereupon we were each offered a glass of Rose's sparkling lime juice - also by appointment to HM King William V. It was a refreshing sip while picking at some roasted peanuts, scanning the walls of the office, covered with photographs, presumably taken with their telescope equipment. They were mainly of the moon and distant nebulae - excellent reproductions. Carlsberg was pleasantly informative, and ostentatiously proud of his new department. Having been down this path before, the two assistants excused themselves and left. Upon their exit, Carlsberg became serious and said,

"I hope you fine people are considering not staying long.", his voice barely above a whisper. Too many WASPs around." he hissed. "That is Western Australia Security Police, as opposed to EASPs, if you know what I mean."

He didn't smile and continued:

"Nobody likes them but they have an aversion to northerners." We nodded and giving thanks left the way we came in and with Dusty driving, exited the university compound and, once more, headed to the highway back to Woomera. Once again it was dark when we reached the base. We packed our newly acquired supplies into MSE-1, using some of the space where the cases had been.

"How long will it be till ready for takeoff?" I enquired of Tom. "About forty minutes. I did major prep and recharging this morning before our trip to Adelaide, so let's have a bite to eat and get ready." And we did. We experienced the inevitable Australian snack - Vegemite sandwiches with cheese and a bottle of Foster's.

With its fuselage at its resting position of about 65 degrees, and both wings in full swept-back position, descending at the same time as the fuselage was ascending, making two points of a three point landing; the third point being the rear undercarriage at the tail. We were facing East in order to take off with the Earth's rotation in order to use whatever slingshot effect we could muster - it was unanimous we should head for the moon to regroup. So, boot up, load up fresh coordinates into the IPS - suit up, zip up and get into a relaxed posture, wait for the two minute countdown, then - 5, 4, 3, 2, 1 - we have liftoff, gradually accelerating to escape velocity of ten kilometers per second.

The take off went without a hitch, just after nine p.m. We didn't find out till much later, that, as we were taking off in a remarkable display of fireworks and thunder, about a mile from the control town, there was a white high performance car, with WASP in black letters above a red stripe on each side of the vehicle, heading for the disused base. It was speeding down the highway, with four not-too-friendly uniformed government employees inside.

As we slowly ascended, this car was about ten minutes away from the old base, racing westwards, directly under our eastbound flight path. I would guess they then turned around, and, disappointed, drove back to Adelaide with less urgency. As soon as we exceeded escape velocity at just over a thousand miles high, we were tossed into what seemed like deep space, and as if by magic, we would tangentially meet the lunar orbit in three days, twelve hours, and five minutes. We would then make one lunar orbit and automatically park ourselves five miles above the LSS. Then we'd revert to manual control. I would glide the craft down and surf our way into the Sea of Tranquility; the geodesic Dome getting bigger and bigger as we came closer and closer to what could be or even may be, a final touchdown

Chapter Five

Dreams Live On

"Mother Knows Best"

THE THREE DAYS, TWELVE HOURS AND FIVE MINUTES it took us to reach our lunar destination seemed longer than the year it took us to reach Mars. Apart from work-related questions, answers and commands necessary to support our relatively simple trip, there was nothing said. I'm sure we shared similar thoughts. Were we fleeing from a sinking ship? Did we have to drown with that ship? It was like we were sailing to some desert island somewhere in the middle of our solar system, where we knew we would meet up with some already shipwrecked astronauts. What to do there - lots, I know. There are labs, workshops, pretty advanced telecommunication equipment, machine ships, very high-tech tunneling machinery, there's teenage kids to teach, medical centre to support, all very well equipped, and all expanding.

There are about 120 living cabins, all connected to the main dome by a labyrinth of pressurized corridors, about two dozen or so Quonset type huts, each hut fifty feet by one hundred feet floor area, used for storing large machine work. There were huge storage areas excavated into the walls of the crater, sealed off and pressurized. There's probably a limited book supply and still no space net, just lots of I Love Lucy reruns.

We touched down and screamed to a deafening halt at the end of a five-kilometre runway; retro rockets blazing, tearing up chunks of lunar rocks and dust. They have this huge Zamboni type truck to smooth out the runway after every landing and takeoff. That operation takes a couple of days - even senior technicians sign up for their turn to drive the truck - talk about little boys and their giant toys. So much fun!

The roar was noisy as hell inside the spaceship, but if someone was able to stand outside and observe the landing, they would hear nothing. But they sure feel the ground rumbling. At the extreme of the runway was a pad where we finally came to rest. This pad was part of a movable roller system, and after a half an hour of cooling we were rolled into a huge, cavernous hangar built into the side of the crater. We opened the airlock and with the help of a custom built ladder, clambered down to luna firma, still wearing our pressure suits.

No more walking, we hopped slowmo to the exit airlock - waited fifteen minutes for the air pressure and content to stabilize - then discarded our pressure suits. There was a well-lit tunnel joining the hangars to the main complex - very walkable, or rather hoppable, and wide enough for two Batmobile type scooters, one of which I opted to use to carry my pressure suit and some personal effects; the rest can come later.

A pair of friendly technicians scurried around, obviously expecting us, and almost immediately started servicing our tired MSE-1. Hope they'll fix our video radio R.T. apparatus. The tunnel led directly to the main geodesic dome. It felt good to be here, no one was sick or war struck or starving: my hunched-up shoulders relaxed as the tension slowly oozed out of my body. That lucky-to-be-alive feeling was returning and this very spacey Club Med felt like home.

There was more green, more birds, and more life under this gigantic dome than there was six years ago when I was here. I noticed two little dogs, Corgis I think playing with themselves while being taken for a walk by a young couple, one male, one female, both about my age - interesting, I think I'm going to like it here. I stopped my scooter outside the commander's office and pushed the buzzer.

"Enter." A guttered growl resonated from a Germanic voice box, as two ceiling-high doors swung open automatically revealing a spacious office area, luxurious and inviting, and,

"Chuckie!" with wildly overt enthusiasm.

"Ziggie!" I bellowed back and we met at a thumbs-up

handshake and embracing hug. Dr. Siegfried von Braun has been the commander of LSS ever since it's inception twenty years ago - yes, it's the same von Braun; Werner was Ziggie's great-grandfather. That's right, the V1 V2 mastermind, the creator of the early Apollo project. His squared of head, brush cut and rimless spectacles only reinforced his Teutonic trademarks, but he had the same eyes, soft and deeply set as his great-grandfather. I met Ziggie on my first lunar trip in 2050, having graduated from Akademie of Astronautic Sciences Hamburg, the previous year. Dr. Siegfried von Braun was one of the original graduates of the original college back in 2035, after which he was the supreme commander of the blossoming Lunar Settlement Expedition.

"Welcome back," he beamed.

"Notice the improvements since your last visit?"

We walked over to an observation deck, and he gestured to some new buildings under construction.

"I'd like to get a nuclear fusion unit there," he winked. "Maybe one day. We have four of those mammoth cargo ships in our hangars, as well as a couple of little buses like yours, and even some smaller ones we use for exploring," he confided. "We've been receiving cargo contents of at least two flights a year for the last ten years - apart from this last year. There's been just one flight since the war, and they sent that one mainly to take those back who wanted to go back, usually because of kids' reasons, but God knows why. When I look at that mother Earth picture, and how the colours have changed in twenty years - the blues are more grey, the greens are more yellow, and those constant clouds…"

"Here!" He threw his arm out in a semicircle. "Here we have ninety-five people, I guess ninety-eight with you three, about ten families with usually one, sometimes two kids of school age. Indeed we have a couple of teachers too. There are about forty single men and a half a dozen single women - one big happy family. Everyone has a job; everyone has a responsibility, and here because they want to be here. We have regular base meetings and support groups where necessary, we have no unsolvable problems Chuckie and we're stocked up for years." He slapped his thighs, gave a broad grin, peppered with a smug, hehehe sound. He gestured towards the Earth and shook his head, "But just watching the old lady getting sicker. Come!" He directed me to a very comfortable reclining chair, went to a closet, and produced a bottle of wine with two sparkling crystal glasses. Tom and Ron were still occupied with landing duties.

"2025 Mission Hill Pinot Noir." he proudly proclaimed.

"Received a couple of cases a while back. They tell me it got all sorts of awards. Here's to your continued good health, Chuckie."

Only two people had called me by that derivative - one was my mother, and the other was Ziggie von Braun. I hadn't thought of my mother for quite a while - was never that close to my parents, but why go down that road right now. She always seemed to have money for music lessons, or extra clothes that I didn't need, and all the books and equipment I did need at age fourteen. She never objected to spending - she was good at that - or driving me here, and there, and sometimes, everywhere.

Sometimes I would get the impression that I was slightly in the way of her chosen life style - expensive restaurants, exotic holidays, and exorbitantly fashionable clothes. Father was away more than he was at home - I think - his government job as a marine biologist would take him either to Ottawa or to some fish farms somewhere off the northern British Columbia coast. I wonder how business is for him these days.

He and I never talked that much. I think he was always afraid I knew more than him, which I usually did. I think he viewed me with a level of curiosity, rather than pleasure or pride - maybe something he had to put up with. Ziggie however, was curious about our recent visit to Earth.

"It's getting to be a pretty sad place, eh, what! No place for an ambitious fellow like you, Chuckie - Captain Charles Chuckie." He was playful but serious, "You're a born leader, my friend. You'd make an excellent lunar commander - when it's my time to quit, that is, but that might take some time, I'm feeling so good." He flexed his well-toned body, easily concealing his fifty-five years and laughed, pointing to me.

"I presume this is some sort of extended visit of which this is the first day. So what do you want to do for the rest of your life? We've been tracking you for a couple of days, wondering what you were up to. Is it too late to save the world - is it worth saving?" He turned and stared silently at the setting earth.

"Do you still have dreams, Chuck?" with a reassuring hand on my shoulder. I nodded. "Dreams live on - we can work it out - dreams live on - dreams live on, and on, and on…"

I continued sipping wine, slipping further down into the body-hugging chair, making sure all parts were supported. I had this irrational fear that I might fly off the chair, to where, who knows… There was only a sliver of earth above the horizon now - soon to be gone - I wonder how long sunup would be. The LSS was constructed in a medium-sized sub crater, stuck on the rim of a much bigger crater, making use of the cooling shadows produced by a rising sun. Apart from four observation decks, the geodesic dome was completely shielded from outside sunlight and abrasive cosmic dust particles. The inside of the dome itself emitted artificial light, electronically controlled to follow a twenty-four hour cycle, so as to simulate earth time, which incidentally was set at GMT.

That wine is sure good - like nectar from the gods. Making me feel all fuzzy and warm - the dome seems to be lifting and now sinking - triangular sections falling around my head - the dome is pressing on me - and now shooting out into space.

Almost at the speed of light breaking up into a million kaleidoscopic glittery triangulations - whooshing by -

blown by solar winds dancing pieces, as if on interstellar space strings - a million cosmic marionettes - in and out and round and round - was I sleeping - was I dreaming - was I conscious - is this a conscious dream - will this dream live on - now I'm feeling heavy and dizzy and heavy and so dizzy - spinning round and round, worse than that super machine - but now comfortable, slowing down - no panic - wrapped up in cosmic strings again - suspended from somewhere in nowhere land - must be a black hole - there is no light, there is no dome, what am I doing am I leaving home? Should I go to sleep? I think I need more sleep. I snuggle further under the bedclothes in order to….where am I…

"Chuckie, Chuckie."

What the hell was that - now where am I? Like what's happening? What's happening - we're crashing…

My mother's firm but gentle hands are rocking my upper shoulder to the rhythmic calling of my name.

"Chuckie, Chuckie, time to wake up, we have to be down at Convocation Hall at one o'clock. Remember. You sure were sleeping deep this morning - talking in your sleep earlier - couldn't understand much - must have been dreaming, eh?"

My eyes were still closed; even with them closed, I could still see geodesic triangles of all sizes and colours. Dreaming? Me? Remember? Oh, yeah - today's the day we have to go down to University of Toronto to pick up that degree stuff; guess I've got to wear that gown thing, then, aloud - "What's for breakfast, mom?", grunting like a tired lazy teenager, which is what I am. After all, this was the absolute last day of school, then summer break - means vege out, right?

I really don't fancy the prospect of lining up with a crowd of twenty-two to twenty-three year olds, all looking kinda dorky and uncomfortable, just to pick up the ceremonial piece of paper, just so parents can sit and glow with pleasure and pride.

"I've got French toast already." The voice of efficiency rang out.

"Oh, mom, you're so multicultural." I hope she missed my sarcastic edge. I opened my tired eyes at last and looked around a familiar room, with one of my favourite books on the bedside table - Across the Space Frontier by Dr. Werner von Braun 1956 edition - a classic.

We met over the kitchen table; the air flavoured with freshly ground coffee beans, maple syrup, and toasting bread. "There's some mail for you from Hamburg, Germany." She pointed at a large brown envelope on the kitchen table. "Is that the space place you've been writing to?"
It was indeed from the space place and inside amongst all the information brochures, was an application form for the Akadamie of Astronautic Sciences.

"They only accept applicants with doctorates," I informed mom after glancing through the package, "Guess that's why I'm going to Princeton University in the fall."

"You still want to be a spaceman, Charles?" Mother stopped her chores, turned, hands on hips, quizzical, and let out a deep, long sigh.

"There are so many things you could be good at you know, like playing cello, like your Dad, for instance. You played good with that string quartet from the music department at the university, and you weren't even studying music there. And you seemed to enjoy it - why don't you practice more." Every parent arrives at this question sooner or later. I mumbled a nonverbal reply. If I was into it, I'd be practicing five or six hours a day and enjoying it - I do enjoy playing music, but I'm usually too busy doing other things, like reading textbooks, writing papers, or helping a fellow student with some school problem.

"C'mon, let's get going, Doctor Rockheart. Did you remember....did you forget...?"

My auditory pathways jammed the transmission of my mother's continual interrogation, developing into a repetitive overuse syndrome.

"Get it together, young man, or you'll never get anywhere, y'know."

"What was she talking about?"

"Come here, come here." She turned me towards her. "Are you living in a dream?" She queried. "Do dreams live on?"

We looked eye to eye as she straightened my tie.

"Sure, mom. My dream lives on. You can be in my dream."

Chapter Six

SURVIVOR

"GALACTOGENETIC NANOFUSION FROM AN ELECTRON TO A STAR"

CHARLES ROCKHEART SLIPPED A LITTLE LOWER, a little lower into his body-hugging recliner. He had a relaxed satisfied smile on his face - the face of a thirty year old. He surveyed the dynamics of the techno-utopia that sprawled out in front; giving a 360-degree view from his glass-walled office; which he inherited from his late uncle Ziggie, before becoming commander-in-chief of the Lunar Space Station. It was he who lead the way almost fifty years ago putting into reality his long-term dream of a vast expansion of the necessary moon base.

After the last great war of 2054, it was obvious that massive changes were on the order book. Millions died during and after that which has become known as the heinous catastrophe of 2054. Government leaders met with all the scientific and technical support available to begin a mega plan for what was left of the planet, and expansion of the moon base. Development of a Mars project would be included in the long-term plan.

Captain Rockheart, or Cap'n, which was how everyone who passed would greet him - had recently returned from a second expedition to Mars. Recently discovered on the red planet were vast underground sources of virtually pure water. This water - mixed with methane evaporates in the hot but short summer season, but when doing so produces usable oxygen - all emanating from huge caves. Much of the preparation and scientific experimenting of almost all of the outer space specimens was carried out at the laboratories at LSS – better equipped than any facility on Earth.

The Moon Base was a huge patch of civilization, bluntly standing out against a relentless moonscape; there were hundreds of kilometers of specialized highway. This "highway" carried automatic transit cars - silent, driverless and guaranteed never to fall foul of an accident. Some branches would lead to huge work areas, sometimes built into the side of mountains, a safeguard against aggressive meteorites. There were four full-sized take off/landing pads, handling up to five flights a day each. The next manned trip to Mars should take between 4-6 weeks due to new fuel discoveries and acceleration techniques - major advances in uses of nuclear fusion - new, clean energy.

The moon side population consists of 10,000 permanent and 15,000 temporary, on a 3 month-on, 3 month-off basis. There are two fully equipped hospitals prepared for major surgery, an ever-expanding school system, and a busy, thriving atmosphere. There are plans for 250,000 people to settle on Mars in the next half-century, and also plans for a manned expedition to Europa, as it encircles Jupiter - an expedition for the next generation. Captain Rockheart has a son and a grandson, both working in the space business: his son is a pilot and his grandson is into software design.

There are lots of recreational and entertaining pastimes on the Moon Base: multidimensional sound and light systems, interactive music studios, theatres, and facilities for all ball games. Advanced medical procedures, nanomedicine, mitochondrial surgery, and psychotropic video screens are all used strictly for recreation - makes the old 3D stereo seem bland by comparison. There are nanophotogramy labs, and through reversed logarithmic acceleration, incredible velocities can be achieved and maintained - sometimes well over 100, 000km/h.

Man has certainly discovered new energies, especially since entering the 22nd Century. However, humanoid decision-making is sometimes not easy, especially when surrounded by the vibes and realities of robotica. But, as they say - go forward, go fast, go strong, but go anyway.

Chuck Rockheart arose smoothly, pivoted himself on his extended elbow, and lightly sprang up on his athletic frame - forgetting for a moment the difference in gravity between Earth and Moon. He flicked his shoulder length hair off his face - must go and meet my son coming back from Earth - more hardware to unload - seems like everything goes through now, straight to Mars.

Charles Rockheart is just a few clicks off his centenary, and sometimes the old body feels a little tired once in a while, but there'll be no more major expeditions for him - let the boy do it, he needs the exercise. After all, Charles did receive the Nobel Peace Prize in 2100 for his commitment and input into the Rehabilitation, Renewal, and Resettlement of all the countries on Earth. But it was the World Bank and other mega rich entities that would only back up the gigantic rebuilding plan on the condition that war was deemed illegal and all weapons put down. There has been not one military death since 2054 when the Universal Arms Agreement was signed by 195 countries (following the end of the Last Great War).

It was Captain Charles Rockheart who, devoid of patronage and patriarchy, was able to bring many sides together back in the day. It was he who over-saw the initial moon trips and the Mars program. It was he who brought justice and peace, sharing and caring, back into government. It was he who only wanted to go beyond Pluto. Soon time will slip by and soon he'll be out there but for now the space train stops at Europa where there was a recent soft landing. The robot pilot has sent information to Moon Base (back to Cap'n C.R). Maybe that's why the Cap'n was smiling - just got the news - there's life on Europa!

What the robots did was to take some methane compound, take it outside the tiny spacecraft, and check its reaction after it's mixed and measured with some unknown chemical compound at almost absolute zero degrees - with incredible results. Definitely chemical and definitely organic producing carbon dioxide coming from the methane compound. But, also showing was an abundance of oxygen being produced from somewhere. Furthermore, the whole mini-plantation (one meter by three meters) was expanding at a rate of knots, so much so that the robot has drawn a Lego-type boundary 10cm high around the little plot. That boundary has become sticky, and is chemically eating its way into the soft rock below, exuding carbon dioxide and oxygen. Is there life on Europa, was there life before the big bang, what do you say Cap'n Chuck?

"As long as you've got some multidimensional processing system, everything should work out just fine", his steel-blue eyes twinkle. "Tread lightly" he said. "Make sure you tread lightly, but avoid the sights and sounds of toxic politics. Be ruled by the tools of economics."

And, you might well ask - what did happen to Chuck Rockheart after he recovered from the first trip to Mars combined with the Last Great War with all its stresses and strains? He took a year on the moon to chill out. Then back to school and Captain Rockheart became Doctor Rockheart, after receiving a medical degree from Harvard. Chuck had always kept a hands-on approach with medical research into all aspects of medical science, using multiple digital sensors and T-cell therapy. Quantitative easing was used in medicine, used in economics, used for everything. Either way an anti-immunomodulated response will be apparent.

His eyes closed. He dreams of studies in transgenics and stem cell surgery. Low gravity seems to be good for the healing process, but does not do much to maintain muscle strength. Chuck looked quite tired as he slowly made his way to his favorite recliner and lay in it, looking up at an endless starry sky. He stayed smiling, as his head dropped sleepily to rest on his chest. He's out there drifting in some nebula.

Wordless, Charles' son left the room, his father to sleep… perchance to dream. He'll never know what might be in store, when he goes where no man has ever been before…

Humanoids keep searching for Anarkey,
Especially when travelling to a star is free.
They'll open every lock they see.

There are more than enough mistakes waiting to be corrected,
Many petty crimes to be suspected.
So stick to the circle, it's the best way around.
Then follow that circular thread.

Touch every aspect, see a mysterious ultrasound.
"Keep following that circle" he said.
"Reach for perfection, choose your direction,
but move until your bones find you dead."

EPILOGUE

WALL STREET JOURNAL, May 10, 2032.

Exxon reports successful drilling deeper than 10 miles at 2 sites in the Yukon, Canada. Boundless geothermal heat energy can be harnessed and converted in estimated ten trillion kilowatt hours per year. Such geothermal drilling has been operating successfully in Northern Manchuria and eastern Siberia for two years.

TORONTO STAR, July 1, 2042.

AP reports first moon baby was born 5 days ago. Mother and son doing well. Details on page 77E.

NEW YORK TIMES, December 18, 2049

After two years of on/off negotiations, the Taiwanese delegation walked out of the China reunification talks in Beijing today. A spokesman said talks were at an irreconcilable breakdown; the Chinese Government conceding to no demands made by the Taiwanese representatives. The entire delegation arrived in Taipei to demonstrations and celebrations of the centennial of Taiwanese independence, so claimed.

WASHINGTON POST, November 11, 2053.

Pyongyang, North Korea, has been encircled by an estimated 20,000-armed insurgents, once again demonstrating the lack of closure following the temporary armistice of 1953, when the 38th parallel artificially divided the North from the South of Korea. Sympathetic riots in Seoul and Pusan were quelled by the South Korean National Guard using nerve guns. Over 50 killed and hundreds injured.

BOSTON TIMES, November 12, 2053.
Two American aircraft carriers, the USS General McArthur and the USS General Eisenhower have been deployed to Okinawa and Kobe, Japan. They will arrive in 2 days to monitor the North Korean developing situation.

LA TIMES, January 1, 2054.
Two Mars bound spaceships successfully take off from the Lunar Space Station, this morning, beginning a 2 year round trip to the red planet.

SAN FRANCISCO CHRONICLE, January 19, 2054.
Satellite pictures confirm massive buildup of troops on the Chinese mainland opposite Taiwan, also intensive naval activity in the Straight of Formosa. The White House has demanded an explanation; otherwise, the recent electric car trade agreement may be in jeopardy.

CHICAGO TRIBUNE, January 20, 2054.
Two American battleships sail at high speed towards Taiwan to investigate…

Chapter Seven

FUTURE FOOTPRINTS

"THE PAIN BEHIND THE TRUTH OF WAR"

LETTER TO A FUTURE EDITOR

Dateline: January 1, 2114

It's almost forty years since the Warsaw Agreement that committed countries of the north and west to pay for the cost of the damage incurred by the still-developing nations and alliances, following extreme climatic disturbances, storms, hurricanes and the like, the size of which was increasing every year, leading to floods, landslides and innumerable human losses.

Meanwhile (back at the ranch) these same rich countries were spending billions of dollars looking for ways to create new energies - so the rest of us could continue to consume with careless abandon. Which is what we've been doing for far more than forty years.

Remember when the wind machines used to produce cheap power - until the cost of the process superseded the savings thereby retrieved from the new energy? Now the wind machines are becoming rusty. Those old-fashioned solar terminals are powerful but terminally sick, probably even the cause of the recent outbreak of SAD.

Average temperature increase through the first half of the twenty-first century has been 4.5 degrees, and rising. The atmospheric carbon dioxide level went way past the danger level twenty years ago. Doesn't the air feel heavier just to breathe it? We don't talk about it anymore, but the oceans are lifeless, and disease is rampant and spreading.

We are grateful that the birthrate is falling - as is, incidentally, general food production. It's almost unbelievable how the human race adapts to change. Especially if it's a matter of surviving…

Did we see it coming? I'm sure we talked about it when you and I were much younger. But those with power and control never seemed to do much about it, apart from adding a few more zeros to the Agreement (probably to the benefit of the rulers rather than to the people of less fortunate countries). Now they tell me there are some better remedies. Can't wait to see them make the climate change. Haven't learned yet what life is for…

It seems we're in some kind of "supertech" time. But you'd think they'd solved a few puzzles by now. Should have spent more time and money looking after the jewel they had before. Twenty-twenty vision sees everything well - especially back in the day. Now nature is running wild. She'll make us pay for all those wrong decisions made yesterday. Perhaps knowledge is not what we need any more, enlightened as we are now in 2054.

- Disgruntled Reader, Toronto.

A GLIMPSE AT RACIAL KILLING (...NEVER AGAIN)

They say we must never forget the holocaust,
>   so we'll know why we say never again.
But it wasn't the first and won't be the last.
>   On some level or other, blood is spilt every day.
Twenty million souls in Armenia would vouch for that.
>   It seems like every century there's an interracial clash.
Muslims hate Hindus, Hindus hate Sikhs, Muslims hate Muslims.
>   Northern Irish Protestants hate southern Irish Catholics.
Even in Africa, Muslims hate Christians.
May a compassionate God help the racial catastrophe that has destroyed
>   Lebanon and Syria.
They hate Russians in Chechnya, from China to the Steppes -
>   they would kill every one if they could.
Let us give some thought to the massacre of indigenous people
>   of Australasia and the Americas, from Baffin to the Falkland Isle.
From the racial strife in Guatemala, in Chile, and in Argentina, massacres
>   abound, often with political motives, but always an initial racial
>   spark would start the fire.

It's usually us against them - am I glad I'm one of us.
In Africa, 800,000 Tutsis were slaughtered in three weeks.

A little further south, the king of all hate - Apartheid.
This was state-controlled separate development
>   of anyone but white - memories of 1984 and Brave New World.
White is often the most despised non-colour, standing apart from the rest.
After all, there are many shades of brown, black, yellow or red.
China can dispose of unwanted minorities efficiently
>   and anyone who doesn't look like the majority (original meaning).
Japan was exceptional, almost conquering the eastern half of Asia several
times.
Japanese hordes with sword and gun
>   made short work of the retreating Chinese millions.

We haven't forgotten the xenophobes in Australia and New Zealand

      when thinking about the treatment of indigenous people by white
settlers.

No refugee boats allowed, let them sink or go to Bali.

      Long live Australia, the only place left where white is always right.

Be aware of the white cousins in the back country of upstate Mid-West USA.

      These would be known as the For rent, Mexicans need not apply crowd.

These cousins would be armed to the teeth and difficult to deal with,

      as was Genghis Khan, ruler of all Asia, for a short time.

He never made it to Africa, a constant scene of racial killing to this day.

There, in Uganda, and in the Central African Republic, including Sudan they'll

      attack a village at night, destroy it with sword and with gun,

      torture and rape.

In Syria they'll attack the ancient city of Homs with machine gun and grenade,

      they'll attack with chemical weapons and then with bombs,

      they forbid access to food, medicine, and water.

They have killed more than 200, 000, made resident refugees of 2 million or
more,

      and a half a million now spread out in neighboring countries.

This civil war is totally racial in origin and nature, pitting families against families,

      royalty against peasantry.

In fact, all skirmishes, battles, and wars have some origin based on race.

Gold, silk and exotic spices are part of the bounty of trade.

But race sets the pace,

      and man will stand supreme pleading,

      please never, never again.

For every death in every war for every mother's grief and pain.

Love often dies but you can't kill hope.

And you keep saying never, no never again.

WHEN IRISH EYES WERE CRYING

Soldiers young and old they fought for Ireland
and both sides claimed the blessing of the Lord,
but if there's a God above, why don't he tell them
they'll never find their peace with bloody swords.

Although a couple of miles from dear old Belfast,
we can still hear the guns firing far away,
and women cry as sons and lovers die there.
Oh God, the sea is red in Galway Bay.

That's when Irish eyes were crying last,
remembering the gunfire from back in the day.

RECESSION DEPRESSION

What recession, what recovery,
    who are they trying to fool again?
What depression, which discovery,
    when we wake up to the real pain?
We still have food and clothes and water
    the Visa bill still comes with alarming regularity.
Still driving to work, to what we oughta,
    everyday is a special singularity.
Much more people looking for much less jobs,
    poor souls dying everyday.
Too late to cry, there's no time for sobs
    will there always be airplanes to fly you away?
There's a trillion or two still in the government banks
    most goods are still made in China.
A CEO on Wall Street quietly gives thanks
    as he delivers an appropriate one liner.
But when there's no meat and the store has no rice
    and you walk like there's some rocks in your shoes.
You know you're not making it and that don't feel nice
    when, for cheques, the Government issues IOU's.
Did I hear you say bread will be fifty bucks a loaf
    five hundred dollars will fill up your tank?
Water or wine, you can't have them both,
    when the global economy just sank.
Recession or depression, it couldn't happen here
    we still got the Welfare, pogey and all.
All they seem to do is give us mega fear
    and still we will come when they call.
They will try to fool us, any way they can,
    they'll try to fool our daughters and sons.
Peasants never had power since the world began,
    and we know who has the money and the guns.

While cash is still king, there'll be options galore,
      with gold past a five thousand an ounce.
Re-adjust your plans and stay strong to the core,
      for they say, pretty soon, back we'll bounce.
Beware manic depression, polarising the past
      discover recovery, God knows will it last.
So, recession, depression which one will it be,
      discovery, recovery, sounds good to me.

REMEMBER THE DAYS

Do you remember the old days? I know I saw you there.
Now nothing much has changed, save the colour of my hair.
We play the same music, drink the same old beer,
      wish the same old folks a same old Happy New Year.

Do you remember the old days when there were no smart cell phones?
Space was sci-fi, no one had heard of clones.
Now the cars go much faster and there's so many more,
      the sky's looking hazy; my eyes are feeling sore.

I remember the old days, the house had no heat,
      just thankful for anything we could find to eat.
Going to the can, early morning in the rain,
      learning the rule - there's no gain with no pain.

I remember the old days, long before the first geek,
      there was cardboard in my shoe so the holes didn't leak.
But looking so cool in the new pair of jeans,
      thought I sounded like Elvis and looked like James Dean.

I remember the old days, when there was no internet,
      we used cool calculators, making it easy to forget.
Never had any money, but always had lots of fun
      now the whole world turns on zero and one.

But do you remember the day when the Brits ruled the waves?
Women didn't vote, black men were made slaves.
Merchants traded in silk, spices and gold
      most babies died too soon to reach forty years old.
A pandemic would wipe out millions or more
      and, whatever caused the end of the dinosaurs?

Magic was blamed for life's mysteries
       when primitive superstitions abound.
So many gods there were to please,
       they didn't even know the earth was round.

I remember the old days for better or for worse,
       making more memories until they'd come with a hearse.
From manically merry to morbidly sad,
       do you remember the old days, the good and bad?

INDIGENOUS INTERLUDE

The glossy brochures don't explain
     how this land is truly a gift for all men.
The natural stock grew strong and brave,
     till the white man would kill nine out of ten.
The survivors were lost in the dream of a wide prairie sky,
     and the scream of an eagle's distant lonesome cry.
But neither a generous social safety net nor some clever lawyer's ancient ken
     could prevent another native suicide in Kingston Pen.
The brochures don't explain.

COMING DOWN OVER YOU

Long before we knew, I loved you from the heart,
there's a part of you in me, in you another part.
Only time will tell you what you need to do.
soon you'll feel the raindrops coming down over you.

There's no one to listen, what we've got to say
but keep your mojo working, maybe moving time today.
Don't lay no guilt on me for what you know you've done.
Rain soon coming on down, it's covering the sun.

I'm coming down over you, I'm coming down over you.

Same old stuff again, that's what they want to do.
Do you see the change, it's coming into view?
Something's coming down, it's over me and you.
It's coming down tomorrow, no matter what you do.

I'm coming down over you, I'm coming down over you.

STOP THE MADNESS

It's a sick old world, getting sicker everyday
have to make a change, make it right away.
Stop the madness, cease the insanity

Can't you hear the world crying out "save me"?
before your wildest, weirdest nightmares may become reality.
This could be the end of any current corporate entity,
and finally profits may benefit humankind
better move soon, can't get left behind.
There may be nothing left but at least it will be free.
So, stop the madness now and cease this insanity.

If an alien landed, what do you think he would say?
Would he realise the mess we'd made, then would he want to fly away?
Would he make a list of what may cause a real catastrophe?
Could he stop the madness, could he cease the insanity?

Politicians promise the earth (if only they had that power)
instead they buy guns to kill daughters and sons,
you know a million may die in a hour.
If disease don't get the rest, starvation likely will,
at last the time has come to pay the bill.
There may be water everywhere, but there sure is less to drink
poison gases fill the air as rotting corpses stink.
I wonder if our alien friend can solve the mystery
of how to stop the madness, and cease the insanity.

If there's no great change by 2015, there will be no looking back.
Too late to be clean, too late to go green
alas and behold, it's the end of the track.

DON'T YOU KNOW

The only way to save the race is sharing what we got
redefine equality - figure who needs what
live without the fear of rule by the gun
something has to change the curve: this one won't be fun

It takes big energy to feed a billion hungry heads
someone did it long ago with just five loaves of bread
seems to me most miracles happened yesterday
so if He comes like they said, what would He say?

Hey Jesus, what d'ya think about China?
Just a quick one liner
do you think they might nail you to that cross again.
Don't you know a thousand died in Tiananmen Square - I saw it on CNN

Muslim Buddhist Christian Jew all kill with Divine right
the rich get rich the poor get poorer - screw the peasant's plight
so if He comes with love and peace spreading mystic charms
will He find out real power still lies in money and arm

Would He make it on the media - will He have style
scorn corruption - embracing sinners with a smile
or would He play on incognito - always in shades
would He solve apartheid - will He cure AIDS

Hey Jesus what d'ya think about taser
nothing seems to phase ya
won't you say how they beam you up and back again.
Don't you know they're firing shots at foot patrols in Bethlehem
and a thousand die in Tiananmen Square - I saw it on CNN

From Gaza deadly missiles look for Jerusalem
and a suicide bomber seeks the marketplace in Bethlehem.

WHO

Who's going to feed the sparrow

Who's going to throw his crumbs outside

Who's going to feed the sparrow

When the rains fall and the cornfields die

and you don't hear the call of unborn children cry, when the rains fall

Who's going to take the kids to school

Who's going to see their shoes are tied

Who's going to take your kids to school

Who's going to free the prisoners

Who's going to know they're locked inside

Who's going to free the prisoner men

Who's going to watch lambs in spring

Who's going to tend the flock with pride

and who's going to hear the nightingale if he were there to sing

Then who's going to feed the sparrow?

NIGHTMARE

What are you gonna do when the well runs dry

the dream has gone, no tears to cry

no-one hears you scream and shout,

what are you gonna do when the lights go out.

What are you gonna do when a hungry morning comes

food's all gone, rats got the crumbs

nobody stops and no-one reaches there

everyone's lost in the same nightmare.

Mostly a geek but sometimes a sneaky jerk

needs a screen to say if you play or you go to work

no water runs when the lights go out

nightmare comes when fear stays about.

What are you gonna do when the lights stay out?

Chapter Eight

FURTHER FUTURE FOOTPRINTS

"A CASE FOR THE END OF WAR"

THE PRICE

Marx was a man with a brand new plan - the best thing for the collective good.

Do it for the state, you're gonna feel great, like a good "Red" should.

But they got rich and we stayed poor

(credit cards don't work no more).

Government guy never tells you why, he just puts up the tax.

Carefully avoiding any revealing facts

a billion here for an airplane there

for tomorrow's nuclear scare.

They'll sell you oil and MSG they'll sell you nuclear muck

PVC and 24D -just to make a buck.

They'll sell you guns and aerosols

now they're selling buffalo balls.

And I don't believe how it happens everyday

the things they sell you and the price you pay.

Turn around, take a second look, can't be real only in a book.

Don't trust everything you've heard, don't you know it's someone else's word

so watch that preacher when he says he's better than the one before

sign your name -you're sure to find the way to heaven's door.

Five hundred souls the other week

must be the truth we seek.

And I don't believe how it happens everyday

the things they sell you and the price you pay.

Madison Ave says a guy should have a custom wife

with sights and sounds, smells and shapes that brainwash his life

bank account hits the skids then she takes away the kids

and I don't believe how it happens everyday.

The tales they tell you, the games they play

the junk they sell you and the price you pay.

SPECTATOR

Man take lesson, learning about disillusion
feel he pressure to prepare for future
trapped and frustrated, convinced everything fated
blame he teacher, nobody making it better
Wasting he talent, wondering where time went
building up stresses, housing dormant illnesses
he turn to Jesus, just in case there's a purpose
failing, resigned, nobody warning in time, nobody warning in time

Man take woman, they do the best they can
soon he expect, forgetting give her respect
fighting closed eyelids, staying together for kids
blame each other, nobody making it better
He win, she lose, no wonder she feel abused
he lose, she win, all kinds of money from him
children grow older, parents only grow bitter
lonely, resigned, nobody warning in time, nobody warning in time

Man take power, ambition driving he higher
make big decisions, paving way for corruption
social improvement makes way for self-enrichment
blame he mother, nobody making it better
Man build weapon to protect his position
fear he rule by, believing people are fooled by
reason he losing, not knowing why button pushing
world resigned, nobody warning in time, nobody warning in time

You control your fate -do you know what's going on
look before too late or you'll just sing a song
spectator sings a song

FEEL THE HEAT

Can't avoid the next catastrophe, nature's next move out of your hands
      and anxiety is the one thing you own.
Daily it gets louder, the rumble from far off lands.
      Tell me how to anticipate the unknown.

      Don't you feel the heat?

Everywhere a summer wind blows the cold away
      affecting all the food you need to eat,
exhausted air burns your throat every time you breathe,
      don't you feel the heat?
Thousand tons of Arctic ice are melting everyday
      ain't nowhere for polar bear to meet.
What's the point and is there any reason to believe,
      don't you feel the heat?

Faster cars and bigger planes make an ozone hole,
      scorching up the earth beneath your feet.
It won't take long to incinerate a billion years of coal,
      then you'll feel the heat.
Man may come and man will go, some say that he sinned,
      some say that his time is soon complete.
Even in December you can feel a summer wind,
      now you feel the heat.

Super storm and mega drought circulate the globe,
      the weather's getting worse with every beat.
Now it's hard to think with a fried-up frontal lob,
      don't you feel the heat?
There may be other issues on which we can lay some blame,

if it's someone else's fault, wouldn't that be neat.
Still the sun keeps shining and the world becomes more lame,
everyday you feel the heat.

Ooh, feel the heat, oh yeah there's fire in the street.
Ooh yeah, somewhere they're blowing up concrete, don't you feel the
heat?

LEGACY

Whatever happened to the fifties - so many things going wrong.
The world falls apart, breaking its heart,
sounding like just another duop song.

Plastics had just been invented, credit was the new icing on the cake.
We didn't have smart phones, iPads or microwave,
and we made all the money we could make.

Went to church twice on a Sunday
justifying our legacy by filling the plate.
We taught the natives how to know our God,
and why only He was great.

We had vinyl LPs and colour TV, jet planes to fly us away.
Living couldn't get much better than this,
we won the war and expected peace every day.

Wasn't life simple and wasn't life good?
Can't remember there being much stress.
But the changes that came from the fifties
somehow turned the world into a mess.

WHAT THE WORLD WOULD BE LIKE

We could bore into the earth for ten miles or more
find all the geothermal power as we get closer to the core.
We'd make heat we'd make light, clean as can be,
we'd even make clean electricity.
No more dirty smoke stacks spewing junk into the sky
we'd kiss all those poisonous emissions goodbye.
If only we knew what was coming down the pike
don't you wonder sometimes what the world would be like?

We'd quit using oil, instead an electric car
glides around silently, both near and far.
We would stop treating plastic as disposable stuff
using plastic for landfill is not good enough.
The use of petroleum by-products would take a dive
many people changing many jobs to stay alive.
Some may take a walk, some may ride a bike,
don't you wonder sometimes what the world would be like?

Why don't we naturally grow food we can eat
instead of putting up with genetically modified wheat?
Get rid of chemicals and additives that just cause disease
and pesticides that also kill flowers and trees.
There's a good diet available, whatever that may mean
when plain simple water costs more than gasoline.
So, if multinational plans would just take a hike
I wonder sometimes what the world would be like.

BELIEF

There's something way out there - way far out - what can it be?

Let it be peace, let it be harmony.

Let it be real, as real as a black hole: like a space for feeding the soul.

You have yours, I have mine, some choose to have none.

Let there be no judgment - different is not wrong.

So pray for the co-existence of everyone.

The only change that concerns aliens or other outsiders - is simply
the nature of the belief.

We won the war,

for all it's worth,

leaving the world tattered and torn.

But look what has happened in the sixty-plus years

since the fifties were well and truly born.

Life goes on and so does death, driven by a spirit breath.

Does death of love produce love of death?

Or is it love of death that happens naturally?

MATTER

I used to play better than I do today

I used to know more than any one could say

I was so good back in yesterday.

The Beatles were great, always top of the charts

Wanna hold your hand they're gonna steal your hearts.

They were so good back in yesterday

So good.

Remember the rallies dancing in the street

Breathing love and peace on everyone we'd meet.

Even you tasted sweet back in yesterday.

Used to be sunshine didn't burn your skin

You never got sick from the air you breathed in

The water was good back in yesterday.

But does it really matter, you know what I mean?

It's only idle chatter for peasants and queens.

Maybe it should matter to fools and kings.

But does it really matter in the grand scheme of things?

Look at man killing man today all over the place

White was not right there's no chosen race

He just slipped from grace back in yesterday.

But does it really matter, know what I mean?

It's only idle chatter for peasants and queens; is it too late to matter?

Is it too late to matter, too late to pray?

It didn't seem to matter back in yesterday.

So will it be AIDS or that asteroid,

Will we see humankind kinda self-destroyed?

Like they said it would back in yesterday.

Does it really matter in the grand scheme of things?

GO GREEN

Find a new way to turn wheels
       Do it today pick up heels
Cut out the flying before it's too late
       The coral is dying at a super fast rate

People are sick and dying
       Feed them real quick before you go to the moon
Don't make the bomb, don't shoot the gun
       War would be less, there'd be none soon
Burning up oil warms up the globe
       Nobody using their frontal lobe

What's going to happen when the water runs dry
       What's going to happen when there is no gas to buy
No milk in the cow, no food in the store
       No knowing how folks survive any more

Can't imagine how my hungry heart would beat
       Lining up for sugar and rice, you're lucky if there's meat
Listen to those pundits advertising no fear
       Bet you one or two bits it couldn't happen here

Gotta keep clean, go green
Need a new act - a change of scene

Keep clean, go green

THE KLAN IS BACK

The Klan is back, the Klan is back
Burn the cross - kill the Black
Hate the Jew - hate the Gay
They'll hate you if you stay on the wrong side of the track.

The Nazis are back; they're cleaning the race
Protecting the white from any differing face
Long live white supremacy
They feel so right they never want to see a multicultural trace.

The Klan is back - they never went away
They're talking to them Nazis every single day.
Converting the poor, the weak and the stressed
Promising security, their way is best.

They'll stay to the right whatever that means
They'll keep the world white; they'll keep the world clean.
But it's their sworn ambition from the extreme far, far right
To keep the Aryan winning the race, and keeping the world real white.

The Klan is back; long live the Klan
They'll show us who is the superior man.

IS IT JUST ME?

Are the days really shorter than they used to be
is the sun shining brighter now the ozone is free
do you know when a minute feels like eternity
are the nights growing darker or is it just me

Is the sky turning bluer -it seems week-by-week
are the birds getting fewer like the fish in the creek
are the words getting truer -that politicians speak
will tomorrow be newer or is it just me

If it's reason you're losing
it's of your own choosing
is anyone lying
do I hear someone crying
Now the coral is dying -what's following SARS
pretty soon we'll be buying a condo on Mars
and man keeps on trying to reach for the stars
doesn't time seem like flying or is it just me

Do I hear someone crying...?

IMPOSSIBLE DREAMS

Used to be we'd recognize a cool green theme
    Now it's looking more like an impossible dream
Used to eat a second piece of apple pie and cream
    Then I started voting for the politically correct team
Used to be believing humans were a race supreme
    And able to survive nature's wild and stormy scream
They thought they'd just make more money with their fossil burning scheme
    But using coal and oil only made more steam
I remember how we shared each current green theme
      And how it all changed into yesterday's impossible dream

We cut the trees every chance we get
    We fish the ocean till the fishing's done
Used to buy green mutual bonds, why, now I forget
    Didn't someone say it all comes from the sun
We used to watch the clouds go rolling by
    Tracking contrails streaking across the sky
Somehow we felt much safer back in the day of way back when
    Before I knew how cruel man was to men
Sometimes the grass is greener than it seems
      The more we reached out for virtual impossible dreams

These are some thoughts of man and the footprint he has made
    Down a self destructive path turning sunshine into shade
Maybe we can harmonize again to a green theme
    Before it, too, becomes an impossible dream

Chapter Nine

FUTURE VISIONS OF CURRENT IMAGES

"A SPECK OF LIGHT"

A speck of light is a star; a star is a faithful sun.

The one life-giver through light and heat.

I am a speck of light, more important than the sun,

but the farthest star is nearer to Apollo than I am

of being complete.

DISCOVERIES

First there was the x-ray then the wonder drugs,
        they took a look and gave us longer lives.
They killed rain forests as well as evil bugs
        making sure a human race survives.
They gave us radio and TV, and all that wild computer stuff.
WWW dot COM dot don't forget the bomb,
        no wonder getting by was getting rough.
                        How they changed history,
                        those twentieth century discoveries.

Paper took five thousand years to find a printing press
        Da Vinci only dreamed of flying machines.
Old time groove slow to move, no need for stress
        no need for twenty four foot video screens.
It wasn't long ago the earth was flat,
        now it's spinning faster every day.
We thought we knew it all and that was that,
        now tomorrow's not as sure as yesterday.
                        They re-arranged you and me,
                        those twentieth century discoveries.

The wheel was round long before Henry's killer car
        drove us crazy driving everywhere.
Burning oil, warming soil, who do we think we are
        you'd think we were a little more aware?
What's happening now that there's no Arctic ice,
        will the water rise above our heads?
We blew it once, don't blow it twice,
        don't get trapped under your beds.
                        Will they save you and me,

                        those twentieth century discoveries?

SONG FOR AFRICA'S SON

Africa's son needs to be fed
buy him a fridge, a waterbed
give him a dream; look at him smile
make him feel good just for a while
trained from youth to avoid the truth, psycho through and through
when melting pot becomes too hot, high tech where are you

Breaking me back just for making the rent
long before payday whole thing is spent
making the bed and cry over bumps
chop down the trees and cry over stumps
we see it all by satellite, so proud of what we see
half the world without a bite and still we gotta have kids

Didn't you know, couldn't you tell
hungry dog rings a bell
heard it before, play it again
same old song different zen.

LUCIFER

Lucifer and me took a holiday on a cosmic sea.
Lucifer told me of a cabaret where we could be,
Lucifer to me was a friend in need,
chasing every star as across the sky we'd speed,
looking for a ball of fire.

Lucifer told me of a heavenly space where angels dwell,
Lucifer showed me how to run the race and feed my shell.
I said, *"Lucifer, I thirst"*, and He gave me wine.
Nectar from the Gods making it easy to climb
looking for a ball of fire.

Lucifer left me somewhere in the dark side of the moon
groping for a light, just a little spark would fill my room.
Gabriel said He nearly took you in.
Go find another sun where there's nothing to believe in,
it's better than a ball of fire.

He said:

>　　*"Meditate, meditate, grow until you will be great.*
>　　*Transcending a thought so fine,*
>　　*conscious bliss is yours and mine.*
>　　*Meditate."*

Lucifer was king of the flying fish in a cosmic sea.
Lucifer would ring any bell you wish like one, two, three.
He hides his head behind every asteroid.
He's not looking for what jealousy destroyed,
He's looking for a ball of fire.

He should meditate, meditate,
grow until He will be great.
Meditate, meditate,
gliding through some solar state.
Meditate.

SPIES

Don't pick the flowers that are growing in the park,
    keep that little doggie on the lead.
Watch how you're playing with your lover in the dark,
    someone's checking every single deed.

Don't claim you're working late tonight and then you don't,
    someone hears the beat of every drum.
Don't say you'll pay your taxes 'cos you know you won't,
    and be careful when you drop that gum.

No secrets, life is fast becoming like an open book,
    everyone knows everybody's plight.
One day we'll look at all the images they took,
    photos made by cameras out of sight,
    recording all your noises in the night.

All made by spies in the skies, watching over you,
    spies in the skies seeing all that you do.
Hundreds of antenna's I could mention,
    droning from Alaska to Ascension.
They see through alibis -

    those invisible spies in the skies.

IF

Were I to make stripped screws stiff
      I'd thread my way through the land of IF.
If I tunnelled my way through the earth,
      would I fall up the other side?
Would I pass another guy coming down
      going on a similar ride?

If they threw a string and tied it to the moon
      would it be a faster way to climb into space?
Would the air become so rare you couldn't breathe it anywhere
      and would those pesky Russians win the lunar race?

If only I could step into a mirror -
      the way Alice did with her looking glass.
Would my world become a game - would it even look the same
      or was Alice just a superficial lass?

If only I could make a loose screw stiff
I`d thread my way through the land of IF.

THE LAWS OF PHYSICS

I wish I was in a real space station under zero gravity conditions;

I'd steer myself around the room with some mini rocket contraptions,

one in each hand fingertip control - I truly would be able to fly.

How come I'm so limited by

       the MIGHTY laws of physics?

I dreamt I was traveling near the speed of light and started going forward in time.

I was in a rocket ship, one hand on the stick and the other with a cool gin and lime.

I fell asleep, had a nightmare to boot, and something out there made me wake up.

It worked out okay but I should have known that I wasn't going to break up,

       like the AMAZING laws of physics claimed I might.

It gets very cold up there in the sky

and they are always telling me how heat rises

but down the centre of the earth it gets hotter than hell.

The SURPRISING Laws of Physics are so full of unexpected twists and turns.

As long as Pressure, Time, and Volume are constant

there'll be a mathematical tool; but you never will fool

       the UNCHANGING laws of physics.

All praise to the INCREDIBLE laws of physics

       may they continue to regulate life.

God forbid they discover any more laws of physics

       Thereby causing unnecessary strife.

SOLAR SYSTEM TOUR

One day I'll play on the red sands of Mars

    and bask in a Venusian summer storm.

On Titan I'll find a methane waterfall

    and Mercury is always unbearably warm.

After an ice storm on Jupiter and a ride on Saturn's rings

    Pluto is so cold and has the darkest climes.

Then at the speed of light, I'll catch some interstellar strings,

    and be back on earth where it's raining most of the time.

A.D. 12010

They had huge prisons in which they housed their crooks
hardwired by genes that today don't exist.
I read about them once in some secret ancient books
some copies the Great Fires must have missed.

Let me tell you about that race from ten thousand years ago,
controlled by a system based on barter
and worshipping a god called Money.
Money became all powerful, desired by those in the know
but rights and freedoms always had a charter,
and everyday felt warm and sunny.

Then warm and sunny became hot and sickly
ninety per cent of living matter soon got fried and died.
The atomic wars brought change more quickly
strange how the pain of change is often denied.

Life as they knew it was quite decimated
there are still forbidden areas out of bounds.
How long it will take cannot be estimated
until seasons more familiar come around.

When will everything be not so automated?
Will we ever get used to universal time?
It all feels so sterile, and even constipated,
        not worth it for a crook to make a crime.

A VIGNETTE OF A POSSIBLE FUTURE

Dateline: Jan 1, 12014

Lunar Institute of Advanced Learning - Annual Assignment

Give a brief report on your recent annual vacation trip to Earth. Describe the recently increasing development of the "methanoids", with relation to the anatomical and behavioural similarities or differences, with current humanoid biped, i.e. Homo Sapiens and Homo Frontalis.

Classic English, dialectic or colloquial, and standard text will be used as a method of etymological expression. A journal of your Earthly activities is expected.

My First Vacation

Well, this is a change indeed. There was a time when the Moon was a favourite destination for the more fortunate earthbound humanoid bipeds, particularly the Frontalis section - the only ones who could afford it. And now, here I am - technical assistant, number one level, one year out of senior development college, my first job, my first holiday.

I'm your average Frontalis, born on the Moon, proud of my gene stream, working there, in the lab, like a happy ant that they used to have in the Earth ten thousand years ago, before the Great Sterilisation Programme that followed the Great Fires. I live in Superdome 23. There are a couple of giant domes just on the dark side of the Moon, some going underground, avoiding those nasty unscreened cosmic rays. I caught the Autocrusier - it zoomed me to the take-off pad in eight minutes flat, a comfortable 100 kilometre jaunt.

There were about 25 of us on the medium sized Cruisemaster, suited up and prepped, and ready for the 20-hour journey to "Mother" Earth (there's confusion in that word "Mother"...). It was my first trip and I didn't know what to expect. I'd seen movies, sensavideos, and felt many enhanced cerebral pseudosensations. On the Moon, there are many flowers and plants growing in most of the domes and daytimes are continually bathed in controlled lighting - to coincide with the night-day sleep cycle on Earth. Every so often I think of that misty, stinky, poison, grey sky Earth. The pain differential should be wild. Hope I can find a radical girl on Earth - they're in great demand this year, I am told.

In flight, we were attended by two of the most charming Sapiens that I'd ever seen. I'd forgotten how strong their upper legs and lower body were - kind of attractive in a strange, almost prehistoric way, and they do seem tall. On the other hand, I am as tall as they are but half my height is taken up by my head. I wonder what it's like to have a small head, large hands and feet, as I adjust the pneumatic pillow behind my tired neck.

A short induced sleep, a quick enhanced breakfast drink, and it's time to land. Super enhanced excitement zone is firing all circuits. I believe we're landing somewhere in north-east Canada. We were escorted to a cruise bus and shipped off to a quaint little place called Toronto. Supposedly our hotel was built on the site of the very first garrison inhabited by colonisers 8500 years ago - someone called King York lived here. I wonder what it meant to be royal. I'm not sure if I believe all that stuff - take it with a pinch, I'd say. Tomorrow we take off for the methane lakes and a visit to a lab on the edge of one of the slimy areas. This visit is the ultimate purpose of the trip.

There seem to be helipads every 500m in this place. You catch a helibus at the intersection, fly to catch another one while in flight, and, in the same way, you catch the Transnational. In what seems no more than a few minutes, they drop you on the helipad right outside the lab. Time flies on this place they call Earth - I can't connect the "Mother" to the Earth, just not natural. Meanwhile, back at the lab - there's nothing but stinky green sludge for miles in every direction, quietly, gently bubbling. There are ancient Quonset-type buildings - the lab, and another with sleeping quarters for six workers. All this on a specially constructed concrete pad about 300m square, at the end of a two-lane speedway. No Homo Sapiens working up here. They couldn't take it - the air is too acrid and heavy for them to breathe - they have no resistance to environmental diseases. We Frontalis types seem to cope with methane gas, sulphur dioxide, and the Teflon-like linings. Genetic origin of course, but don't ask us to do anything athletic or strenuous. We just don't have that muscle power. But brain work - we got that together.

The inside of the lab was a stark combination of dull silver and clinical white, clean and bright. The lab techs on duty were efficiently performing their tasks. It was good to see a Frontalis doing some honest work for a change. We filled the lecture demonstration room, which was mainly occupied by a stage on which there was a large glass tank full of the bubbling sludge. There was an added compartment whose content remained well hidden. A 3D screen would facilitate absorption of hypersensitivity and direct comprehensive delivery. The very clean extra compartment was closed off from the main tank by a moveable shutter. The lecturer gave us a rundown on the early biological changes that brought about the existence of the methane lakes - dry stuff, really.

He finally got around to talking about the most recent experiments - observing and investigating the behaviour of - he called them "methanoids". We took turns to look closely at the activities taking place in the extra compartment. The attachment was squeaky clean, corners and all. No slime there, but through the shutters and filters, at the touch of a button, hundreds of little insects one to five centimetres long tumble onto the compartment floor. The little ones were crawling; the big ones were unsteadily walking a few steps and then falling over - accidentally crushing two or three of the small ones in the fall. Half a dozen of the larger ones would group together, and partially separate, to start what looked like a rumble - a free-for-all fight, and (guess what), the biggest ones win, and get to eat the dead little ones (Darwinian). They looked so strange, standing up - their heads half their total height, and disproportionally huge hands and feet, and look, they have four fingers and a thumb on each of their four limbs. The lecturer glowed with pride as he said "This is the Advanced Enhanced Methanoid Development Programme".

He said, "We have a bigger tank with more and bigger

methanoids and we are starting to train them to do tasks and to follow commands". I said, "What! You mean, just like a lab tech?" (The lecturer did not think that was funny, and gave me a withering look as a response). I don't think I want to come back here again. It's full of aliens here. Take me back to the home I know and love, where the food is dynamic and the girls are radical.

After a short tour of the lab and environs, including a relaxing ten minute pre-programmed lunch break, we caught a helibus back to the city area and our hotel. I have to admit that there's no joy in this synthetic food experience. The helibus system is like a complicated highway network, like they had in the ancient times. There are magnetic tracks, parallel, convergent and divergent. Some vehicles carry up to ten people, with a speed limit of 100km/h. These tracks spread out around urban areas, but always join up easily with a superbus, which carries up to 50 people, at a speed up to 300km/h - totally silent and completely pre-programmed. No accidents on these roads. We travelled on a mega superbus to a main city exchange, where we transferred to a mid-sized helibus.

The next day was for sightseeing. After a couple of transfers, we travelled west as far as we could and joined a southbound track, cruising at about 150km/h east of the Rocky Mountains (and did they ever look rocky!). No one goes west of the rockies: there's nothing there, following the earthquakes and the Great Fires from thousands of years ago. In fact we were advised to stay inside until we returned to our original city exchange. No persuasion needed there, dude! It looks horribly uninviting out there - complete desolation as far west as we could see -cold and lifeless - with paler shades of grey and brown.

When the superbus would stop for a passenger to alight at an exchange, we were able to experience the outside conditions - negative sensory overload there. The air was so heavy and warm, with a strange smell of rotting vegetation pervading everywhere. Must get really uncomfortable on an ongoing basis. We were impressed with the speed that the Earth bound residents, Frontalis and Sapiens were maintaining, even carrying out normal daily activities. I knew the Sapiens had a reputation for being strong and quick, but even the Frontalis seemed always in a hurry. On the other hand, we lunar Frontalis type found simple ambulation very tiring, and forget walking up stairs. We were certainly aware that the gravity was six times as strong as what we were used to.

We spent a couple of days doing tourist things, like smell and sound sampling machines, sensavideo centres, virtual and real food experiences, that sort of thing. Got bored after a day or two of being pneumatically stimulated for many hours non-stop, and getting homesick for those lunar comforts of daily living and some clean air and water (the things we take for granted). Couldn't wait to leave that sterile, speedy, and constantly cloudy environment.

The flight back was uneventful and relaxing. Got into a couple of new sensavideos, munched my way through an unending supply of tasty delights, almost until the pilot announced we were gliding smoothly on our final approach to the lunar launching pad. The landing was perfect, as always. We then boarded a superbus to the underground exchange where we gave up those thick pressurized flight suits for normal lunar attire. We then went through a kinaesthetic exercise routine to get used to normal gravity again.

I noticed two unusual packing cases on arrival at dock 3. One of the technical assistants told me they arrived yesterday direct from Titan on one of the larger transport rocket ships - back from another exploratory expedition to that mysterious Jupiter moon. Being inquisitive, I asked the technician what was up. He explained that because of the general solar system rise in temperature, the previously frozen lakes and methane rivers on Titan had completely thawed over the last 2,000 years. Explorers were then able to discover similar amino acids that originally sprinkled the Earth and other planets millions of years ago. There was a nitrogen-carbon dioxide atmosphere like Mars used to be - with increasing traces of oxygen. Small plants and fungi abound. In fact, the technician said the packing cases contained samples of them - still growing, and also samples of insects - which lived in the methane lakes and rivers, and had started living on dry land, developing some mammalian characteristics. I couldn't believe my ears when the technician told me that these insect samples were similar to the original Earth bound "methanoids".

I walked away stunned. My next vacation will be on Mars. I wonder what surprises we'll find there! At least there are no "methanoids" there … yet.

Martian Daily Monitor
Universal Transmission
Jan 1, 12014

Mass exodus of giant transport rocket ships arriving and leaving Earth's orbit, to and from Moon and Mars settlements. After an unusually warm, wet Earth winter, where the local temperature through the Arctic topped 90F, apparently facilitating a tremendous increase in the number and size of giant "methanoids". They are growing almost two metres long, their head size half of their length. They eat anything apart from plastic and its derivatives. There are billions of them over-running the West World and the North World. Equatorial areas are scorched lifeless and it is thought that the methanoids will remain in the northern climes. However, there is no scientific basis behind this claim - which is thought to be politically motivated. There are fewer than 40 million Homo Sapiens eking out an existence in what's left of the South World. Expansions are immediately taking place in all Martian settlements, to accommodate any residual Frontalis from Earth.

Is this another infrastructure scam? It sounds like the biggest one the Solar System has ever seen!!

www.mdm.com.ma.spacenet

AFTER THE LAST GREAT WAR OF 2054

They didn't expect an earthquake rated ten on the Richter scale
to be caused by the first neutron bomb.
Couldn't have foreseen the carnage and how the infrastructure would fail
or where such destruction would come from.
A mountain range slipped into the sea along with ten million souls.
No time to consider whyfor.
Disease and starvation killed most of the rest, few found survival roles
after the Last Great War of 2054.

It took just another three weeks and fifty million or more had died
from Washington to Tel-Aviv.
The Chinese coast seemed to lose the most, like the whole country was fried.
No wonder there was no time to grieve.
Then they came from the south like lemmings searching for the spoils of the
game
but there was nothing left in the store.
Mutations were rife and humanoid life would never be the same
after the Last Great War of 2054.

Nothing grew right under poison rain especially in the northern climes
the sky was a constant haze.
Australia was clean though hotter than hell but still something like the old
times.
Could it possibly be the next phase?
The bugs are increasing both big and small - they must like the climate change
as out of the cracks they pour.
It was hard to predict how normal became just another shade of strange
after the Last Great War of 2054.

We left the space station about two years ago
and soon saw some flashes on the screen.
Now the first men on Mars are returning, with a month to go,

cruising in a manual machine.
Houston's gone and all we hear is an intermittent radio beam.
Nothing works like it did before.
We're safe so far, soon we'll wake up from the dream we had
after the Last Great War of 2054.

The second ship landed in a pile of Martian dust, the tail fins bent way out of
shape.
Nothing will rot there and nothing will rust - from there would be no escape.
They had a year of water and emergency supplies,
no use to them any more.
They'll never know how earth met its demise
after the Last Great War of 2054.

I was lucky to be part of a genetic enhancement plan, for space IQ 250 was
enough.
I wonder with fear what has happened to man?
Survival has to be rough.
Homeward bound without help - we can land this tin box
laden with specimens galore.
But who's gonna care about our little red rocks
after the Last Great War of 2054?

The closer the earth came, the worse it did look - huge stretches of desert
remain,
Indian Ocean was tempting but then we looked and chose the Nullabor plain.
Coastlines changed beyond recognition - the tsunami was 50 feet or more
reshaping a world stained by nuclear fission
after the Last Great War of 2054.

We touched down near Woomera. There was no-one left on site,
at least there was a little welcome shade.
Some crazy looking sunburned freaks said we should travel at night,
suggesting we should make for Adelaide.

They sold water from an artesian well, dehydrated food became a bore
the shoreline crumbing - soon there's nothing to sell
after the Last Great War of 2054.

Everyone seems sickly with sores on the skin, engrossed with menial tasks,
dazed and kinda spacey, there's no race left to win at hand.
Could this be the ultimate last stand?
Can't eat the ocean fish there's no more northern food
- wondering what this is all for.
I've been to Mars and back- what's left for an average dude
after the Last Great War of 2054?

They fought over water, they fought over oil - they killed for a gram of cocaine.
Then they threw them in prison, left them to spoil, never seen or heard of again.
They traded lives for diamonds, lands for a little gold,
paper money long outside the door.
But power won't be bought and freedom won't be sold
after the Last Great War of 2054.

They talked about changing many years ago,
they always had keys to what it would take to survive.
Get rid of hunger, poverty and disease,
no need of them for man to survive.
No racism or nationalism would be power for the course.
No current realities based on ancient folklore.
There must be rule by an intelligent objective peaceful superior
after the Last Great War of 2054.

LISTEN

I told you what was right was right, you didn't listen
You chose to go about your merry way
Oblivious of falls and trips that happen,
An accident looking for a place to stay.
You'd think you'd want to know about what you're missing
You'd think you'd show some smarts before the fact.
I told you strong and still you didn't listen
Seems to me you should know how the cards are stacked.
So I told the king and yet he wouldn't listen
Intent he was on keeping warm the queen
With no idea of what could be his mission
Or why the palace air appeared unclean.
The royal water is now just a trickle
And certainly not good enough to drink
There is no oil, so nothing to recycle
And the mercury makes it hard to even think.
So now you spend your time just reminiscing
Of a bygone age when everything was funny
I told you a million times you didn't listen
You only wanted to follow the money
So now you're realizing it's too late
Is that why your eyes begin to glisten
A new reality is your inevitable fate
I tell you now and hope you start to listen.
You didn't listen even long ago
How can you stand to hear me say I told you so.
Now you know the future's looking bleak
you even heard Margaret Atwood speak,
and still you didn't listen.

It's just a touch of reality.

DIDN'T YOU SEE IT COMING?

DEDICATED TO THE MEMORY AND DREAM OF FARLEY MOWATT.

ABOUT THE AUTHOR

JOHN LINNELL

A man of music, passion, poetry and storytelling who reaches out to the caring heart and to new discoveries of space and inner wisdom.

For over four decades, in countries near and far, he has sung and played his songs to welcoming audiences.

Books by John Linnell

(Available from Kindle and Amazon)

- *Stories of Life, Love and Loss*
- *Man in Space - A Short Account of War, Space Travel and the Future of Us All*
- *Dark Times - Radical Perceptions of Everyday Issues*
- *Visions: Viewed from Beyond the Ether*

www.ingramcontent.com/pod-product-compliance
Lightning Source LLC
Chambersburg PA
CBHW081205170626
46813CB00010B/3331